SNOW DARK

Susan Bowman

Cover design by: Susan Bowman

Printed in the United States of America

This work is dedicated to all the readers who look at a description in a book and see something completely different. Without you, Lorelai never would have been born... and she thanks you.

CONTENTS

PREFACE

This book came into being when I saw a post asking what the description of a certain princess sounded like. Knowing she was based on the Grimm brothers stories, I quickly began planning a dark version of the character. As I continued my exploration of the character, I began researching vampire myth beyond those normally used and discovered Ambrogio. I took the original Grimm brothers story, and my newly discovered myths to create something new. I hope you enjoy the story as you enter the world of Snow Dark.

CHAPTER ONE

'Once upon a time, there lived a kind and beautiful Princess, her lips were red as blood, her hair as black as ebony, her skin as white as snow.'

A smile crossed Lorelai's lips as she read the first line of the children's book she held in her hands, not a happy smile, not even a friendly smile, but a cruel smile, full of victory. She allowed the book to fall from her hands and it fell gracefully back to the shelf with a plunk, falling over on the shelf, now forgotten.

Lorelai looked around the room, people wandered up and down the aisles of the book store, searching for books to escape their reality, little did they know her kind had used them for centuries to spread misinformation, to change the views of the populace and to alter the course of history. Sometimes it was as easy as creating a child's storybook.

Lorelai watched the people for a while longer, enjoying the smell of the warm blood they all exuded. It made her mouth water, but now was not the time for a meal. She slowly walked back to find the forgotten storybook. She retrieved it from the shelf and walked to the checkout counter.

The young woman at the checkout eyed the book as she was scanning it. "Aww, buying for your daughter?" she asked innocently, looking at the picture on the front. "You look just like her." She laughed.

"No." Lorelai replied.

"Cousin?" The clerk continued to question as she wrapped the book up and placed it in a bag.

"Little sister?"

"No."

"Neighbors kid?"

"No." Lorelai said, annoyance creeping into her voice.

"Boyfriend's kid? Come on, I know it's not for you."

"No, I'm a collector."

The clerk looked confused and wrinkled her nose. "But this one isn't special."

"Oh, but it is to me." Lorelai grabbed her bag, annoyed by the questioning. She would never get used to how nosy these younger humans could be.

"Well, have a good evening." The clerk replied, clearly confused, studying Lorelai's face and then looking at the bag.

Lorelai sighed, this young woman was a nuisance. Lorelai turned and walked out the door. The sun was down by now, the streets were pitch dark, but Lorelai could see as well as if it were broad daylight. She was hungry, she mused to herself, and the store would be closing soon. Perhaps a little snack wouldn't be the worst thing.

Lorelai sat on the bench outside of the bookstore and retrieved the book from her bag. She waited patiently as the patrons all finished their purchases and left. Finally, the young clerk closed the door, locking it behind her. Lorelai stood up, she slowly walked to her.

"Could you help me with something? I seem to have dropped my keys and I can't find them. Do you have a flashlight?"

The clerk nodded, intrigued by the woman. "Let me get out my phone, I can't believe you don't have one. Where were you?"

"I was taking a shortcut through the alley. They must have fallen out of my pocket."

The clerk walked slowly into the alley, the flashlight from her phone illuminating the ground. She was focused on the beam, she didn't even notice Lorelai slowly walking behind her. As they came to the dumpster, Lorelai grabbed the clerks arm.

"I've found what I was looking for." The clerk looked at her in shock as Lorelai moved closer.

"Um, I don't understand. Did you find your keys?"

Lorelai laughed. "No, there are no keys."

The clerk looked uncomfortable as Lorelai moved closer, their bodies were brushing against each other now. "I think I should go..."

Lorelai held tight to her arm. "But you have exactly what I want." She replied low and seductive.

The clerk giggled and peeked through her lashes at Lorelai. "I've never tried anything with a woman before."

"There's a first time for everything." Lorelai said as she leaned forward. The clerk closed her eyes and leaned toward Lorelai. Lorelai grabbed her chin with her hand, then shoved her face to the side as she sunk her fangs into her neck. The clerk whimpered at first and then relaxed and moaned in pleasure as Lorelai drank fast and deep of the warm blood.

She was delicious, young and vital. If she hadn't been so annoying, she might have kept her around to snack on. Lorelai drank her dry, then dropped her to the ground, uncaring. Her name badge on her shirt catching the light. 'Journey' even her name was annoying.

"Well, Journey, you shouldn't have been so nosy, but there's only one place you'll be journeying to now." She laughed as she tossed her raven locks over her shoulder and walked away. She picked up her bag, then peeked around the corner to make sure she had no witnesses to her little snack. A passerby might have thought the two went into the alley as friends, but her coming out alone could cause alarm. Fortunately, the evening streets were empty. Lorelai headed home, satisfied with her nightly adventure.

Lorelai walked into her apartment, kicked off her shoes, then walked to her bookshelf and placed the new addition to her library on the empty book stand.

"Oh, Queenie, how they hate you." She said out loud to the book. "If they only knew that you were the one who could have saved them. But it's too late now." Her eyes glowed in the moonlight as she looked out the window. Her smile triumphant, soon she would wake the rest of her kind and they would feast on the humans they had been cultivating all these years.

CHAPTER TWO

The morning news flashed on the television screen, 'BREAKING NEWS, woman found dead in alley, throat slashed open, no witnesses, no leads'. The reporters droned on, but the woman no longer heard them. She had awakened. It was time for the hunt to begin... again.

For centuries Marie had hunted her prey. Across continents and oceans, creeping ever closer, but her prey was always elusive. Finally, she had gotten reports of murders, always the same, throat slashed open, no blood in the corpse. They had led her to this little town in upstate New York, close enough for a short travel to the big city, but far enough away to be secluded.

Marie still had no idea where the nest was, but maybe this time she could find it, so she could finally kill the Vampire Queen once and for all. She could free all the souls the Queen had enslaved. She would finally have vengeance for the lives of her family who had been taken from her, justice for becoming the creature she had to in order to stop the vampires.

"Lorelai..." The name grated between her teeth as she remembered that fateful day so many years ago.

1150 AD

Marie had always thought her grandmother was crazy when she spoke of the vampires and her families duty to destroy them. Vampires weren't real, just an old myth to scare children. Then that night as they brought in the animals to the barn, she had appeared. Lorelai. The embodiment of evil, in a shell of beauty.

She had attacked Markus, Marie's husband, first, her grandmother had tried to defend him. Her frail body swift with weapons Marie had never seen, but age was not her friend, soon her broken body flew across the yard and smashed into the building.

With her dying breath, she had begged Marie to take up her weapons, destroy the Queen, to end the enslavement of those she had taken as followers. Marie picked up the weapon from where it lay next to her grandmother. She turned in time to see Lorelai descend on her husband. Her teeth sank into his neck as he locked eyes with Marie.

"I love you." He mouthed as the light left his eyes, he slipped to the ground. Lorelai smirked at her as she awkwardly held the weapons, tears streaking her face as she looked at her only family, dead on the ground. Rage filled her as she launched herself at the demon before her, slashing with the weapons.

The demon danced out of the way of her attack, amused that the untrained human would dare to face her. Marie saw a small dribble of blood slowly make its way down the demons face, one last remnant of Markus. As the demon whirled toward her, Marie struck out and connected, blood spattered across her, the ground and Markus's lifeless body.

There was a gurgle and a gasp, the demon held her hand to her throat as the black ooze she called blood continued to pour out. A look of shock on the beautiful, pale face. "Your life is forfeit." The demon had croaked out as it stumbled toward her. Marie stumbled back, tripping over Markus's legs, landing next to him, her silver cross slipping from within the neckline of her dress, sparkling in the moonlight.

The demon hissed and shrieked, disappearing into the night. Marie turned to Markus, gathering him into her arms, crying over the man she had loved with all her heart. She knew the creature would be back for her, so she made a heartbreaking decision. She would leave her home, she would find out everything she could about this creature, then she would destroy the one who had taken everything from her.

Marie adjusted her backpack as she slipped into the trees at the edge of the property. The glow from the burning buildings casting shadows on her retreat. She had placed her grandmother and husband in the building before setting it on fire, hopefully covering the truth of their grisly deaths.

For years she had wandered, never stopping long in one place, going from church, to temple, to repository, always searching for the answers to the mystery of the creature that had attacked her family. Finally, she had come to the door of an old apothecary, the ancient man inside claiming knowledge of her questions, and a way to help her battle her demons.

His eyes riveted on the vial she now always wore around her neck, a vial filled with the putrid blood of the demon. Together they had worked to create a potion of eternal life, made from the blood, but distilled and crafted so she would not change to become the blood sucking monster she hunted.

It had taken months, but at last they had one dose, one chance to turn her into the savior of humanity, and in the light of the full moon on All Hallows Eve, Marie ended her mortal existence and became the Huntress.

Marie shifted on her feet, shaking her head, returning to the present. Even after all these years, the pain of her torture still persisted. Her mutilated feet the only evidence of the pain she had been made to endure. Soon she would find her prey. Finally, this horrible existence would be over.

CHAPTER THREE

Lorelai's raven hair blew in the wind as she drove the convertible through the countryside. She wore no seat belt, even though she drove as fast as the car would go, but why would she obey the mortals laws? She had no fear of injury.

The tires squealed around another corner as she sped toward her destination, crossing the border of the compound, setting off the alarms. Gravel flew as she pulled up to the main building, an unassuming farmhouse in the middle of a huge field. The alarms were set at a frequency that only her kind could hear, but the humans were oblivious to, along with so many other things.

As she opened the door to the car, she stretched from her long ride. The door to the farm house swung open and a short man walked out. His face was pulled into a constant scowl, remnants of an old injury rather than disposition. "My Queen." He bowed.

"Why so grumpy?" She quipped. He rolled his eyes, the joke had gotten old over the centuries. It had even been immortalized it in that foolish book she was so proud of, centuries of telling and retelling from her original version, from the dark version, closer to the truth, humans had taken the tale and made it their own, now it was beloved by children. He snorted in disgust at the thought of his portrayal.

"I'm not even that short." He muttered in disgust as Lorelai walked away.

They entered the building, another short man appeared, carrying a large glass full of a dark red liquid. "My Queen." He said, raising the glass to Lorelai.

"Ah yes, I am parched but I would prefer it from the source." Lorelai walked across the room to the large bookshelf and pushed the secret button, opening a doorway, revealing a set of stairs that went deep into the darkness.

The two men followed her as she descended the stairs, the sound of whimpering and soft crying reaching her ears, causing her to smile. Good, they had supper waiting. Lights turned on as she continued down the stairs, finally revealing a large room, connected to many other chambers.

Lorelai could feel the hundreds of souls beyond those doors, sleeping, waiting, but for now all she cared about was the man bound in the center of the room. He had bite marks on his arms and legs, evidence that her minions had fed on him, they would do this regularly with the most tasty humans. They were like cattle to them, continually milked until the body no longer would replenish itself.

Lorelai looked into the man's eyes, they were haunted and dark. He had seen too much, he knew their secrets, and he knew he would never leave this room alive. Lorelai ran her finger along his jaw as he shivered in disgust.

"Get it over with." He gritted out. "Let me die."

"But my minions like you this way, and I only want a little taste." She purred at him. He spit at her, the liquid running from her eye, down the side of her face.

"Go to hell."

"Oh, foolish mortal, I could have let you end peacefully, for your service to me, but now you will suffer." She looked at the two men who had followed her, as well as the five others who had joined them from the other rooms. "Finish him and have your fill." She hissed as the men's eyes glinted in the light. Screams filled the chamber as the sound of ripping flesh and the smell of blood filled the room.

Lorelai fumed, was there only one human for sustenance? Her minions had been lax in her absence. She heard the sound of the body being removed from the room, taken up to the surface to the pig pens for disposal.

"My Queen, this way, we have others." One of the men led her to another room, where multiple humans were kept, locked away, cowering in their prison. Lorelai sighed.

"This is not the way we keep our food." She said sharply, grabbing the nearest one. "Once I have had my fill, I will remind you of my standards." Her eyes were dark as she ripped into the neck of the man she held, blood spattered her dress, but she didn't care. The cries from the humans making her even more ravenous as she dropped the body she had drained, focusing on an older woman.

When she had drank her fill, she turned to the man. "Destroy them, then come upstairs, we have much to discuss."

"Yes, my Queen." He said, bowing. He called his brothers to help him finish the humans. Blood coated the floor and the screams quickly died as Lorelai climbed the stairs alone. The little fools had made a grave mistake. By keeping hostages instead of willing donors, they could bring the Huntress straight to them.

She would notice the missing people, she would track the signs, she would find them again. Lorelai grew weary of this constant battle. Every time she awoke, the Huntress was there. The fool had cursed herself to eternal life, bound to Lorelai through Lorelai's own blood. While she lived, so did the Huntress.

Nothing Lorelai did could kill her. But she enjoyed torturing her. Lorelai laughed at the memory of strapping red hot metal shoes to her feet and making her dance at her wedding. She should have found a way to kill her when she had the chance, but Lorelai was foolish herself, she enjoyed watching the woman suffer.

She would never make that mistake again. When she finally caught this Huntress, she would find a way to destroy her once and for all. The Huntress was cunning, she had learned much over the centuries, but she did not know everything and that would finally be her undoing.

Lorelai sighed as she removed her soiled clothing and

stepped into the shower, washing away the stench of the humans. It was time to gather the sacrifices and wake her coven.

CHAPTER FOUR

The moon lit the night on All Hallow's Eve, Halloween they now called it, but this night had been given so many names, like herself. The music filled the air, spilling out the door to the night club, she could feel the beat in her body.

Lorelai looked down at her costume, a small bit of humor on her part. The blue and yellow dress blew softly in the breeze, she had cut her long black hair to her chin, she looked every bit the storybook princess.

Lorelai slithered into the club, weaving her way through the dancers, the atmosphere of the party infectious. She could gather many tonight to lure back to the compound.

"Hey Princess, wanna dance?"

Lorelai turned and looked at the muscular man behind her, his shirtless fireman costume showing off his toned abs and tanned skin.

"Well aren't you just a snack?" Lorelai said, running her eyes up and down his body.

He moved closer to Lorelai and whispered seductively in her ear. "Baby, I'm the whole damn meal." He grabbed her hand and led her from the dance floor, Lorelai willingly followed. When they came to a small broom closet, he leaned in for a kiss. "What do you say baby?"

Lorelai kissed him and maneuvered them through the door. Soft sounds of movement could be heard from inside, then the door opened and Lorelai emerged alone. She wiped the edge of her mouth with the tip of her finger, then popped it into her mouth.

"Yes you were." She purred satisfied. She slowly walked

away, savoring the last taste of him on her tongue. As she stood at the doorway, scanning the dance floor for her first sacrifice, she froze. A hooded figure melted into the crowd and a soft familiar scent wafted toward her. It was her own blood.

"The Huntress, she's here." Lorelai thought to herself. She strode across the dance floor, looking for the hooded figure. Finally, she saw her, Lorelai walked up to the figure, grabbed the hood, baring her fangs and preparing to fight. She pulled the hood back and hissed.

"Easy lady, back off you creep." The dancing man said to her as he turned back to his partner. Lorelai grabbed him by the shoulders, looking deep into his eyes. "You will do everything I say." She said, compelling him and sending him to the compound. His angry date turned on her.

"What do you think you're doing?" She asked pushing Lorelai. Lorelai grabbed her next and sent her after her date, but her actions had caused a stir, Lorelai knew it was time to go. Angrily, she swept past the dancers and out the door. She had been there, Lorelai knew it, she was trying to stop her from gathering the sacrifices to wake the others.

"Where are you going, Your Majesty?" Came a familiar voice behind her. The Huntress! Lorelai whirled, her eyes dark and deadly, fangs bared. The Huntress held her weapons at the ready, each designed to kill a vampire.

Lorelai eyed the baton in the Huntress's hand, solid silver, with wooden spikes at each end, designed to break off in the vampires body. Any part of that weapon would cause her pain. She would have to be swift. As a blur, she leapt toward the Huntress, fingers curled like claws, ready to attack. The Huntress blocked with her baton, the silver burning Lorelai's hands, she hissed loudly.

The Huntress pushed back, knocking her over a garbage can, the contents spilling onto her dress. Lorelai growled, watching as the Huntress twirled the baton, angling the spike toward Lorelai's chest, a taunt and a warning. They were both tired of this ancient dance, but unlike Lorelai, the Huntress was prepared for both of them to die.

They circled each other, each landing blows on their opponent, each showing signs of the battle on their bloodied faces. Lorelai rushed forward, her anger distorting her reason. She bared her fangs, hissing at the Huntress, lashing out with her claws, but always her foe danced out of reach. She hissed as the Huntress connected with her side, the spike penetrating slightly, burning as she spun away.

She ripped the wood from her side, rage filling her. She would not lose! Even after all the centuries hunting each other, this Huntress was a child to her, and she was a Queen.

She kicked out, catching the Huntress in the stomach, causing her to fly back, landing heavily a few feet away. Lorelai moved in again, this time she would finish her. Lorelai brought her foot down on the woman's ribs, hearing them crack, smiling with satisfaction. She grabbed the woman and began punching her in the face, reveling in the sickening sound each blow made. She was ready to finish her, she would kill her the way she had destroyed so many of them. She picked up the baton from the ground, the silver making her hand sizzle, but she ignored the pain.

"Put your hands in the air!" The policeman shouted as the red and blue lights of the patrol car lit up the street. Lorelai turned on him, ready to attack. A second car pulled up alongside, the officer springing to action, aiming his gun at her torso. "I said put your hands in the air."

Lorelai hissed and turned back to the Huntress, who groaned, fighting against Lorelai, falling back to the ground in exhaustion.

"Last warning, put your hands in the air or we will open fire."

Lorelai moved toward the officers, growling loudly. The Huntress struggled to her feet attempting to defend the humans.

Bang, bang, bang. The shots rang through the air, Lorelai felt them connect with her body, ripping through the flesh, lodging in her chest. Lorelai raised an eyebrow at the officers and stepped forward, grabbing the Huntress, holding her in the air. She heard the sharp intake of the Huntress as bullets found their home in her as well.

More patrol cars arrived on the scene. Lorelai threw the Huntress down disgusted. There were too many humans, she was not strong enough after her long sleep, she needed to heal and feed. Like a wounded animal, she scurried away, to find a safe refuge to heal and plot her revenge.

"We need an ambulance on the scene," one of the officers radioed in, "gunshot wound." He hurried to Marie's side. Looking at the damage the creature had inflicted. "What was that thing?" He whispered.

Marie pushed him away. "I'm fine."

"Ma'am, you've been shot and beat up pretty bad. We have an ambulance en route."

"I have to go." Marie said weakly, looking into his deep blue eyes.

"You need to rest." The flashing lights from the patrol cars reflected on his name badge, drawing her eyes. 'M. Hunter'.

"M?" She said dreamily, as blood loss made her groggy.

"Mark." He replied as she passed out in his arms.

CHAPTER FIVE

Marie swirled at the edge of consciousness, continuing down until she reached the bottom. The pain resonating through her body. "We have tried so many variations, but every one leads the subject to fully change, I do not see how we can grant you the gifts you desire without you becoming a full fledged vampire my dear." The voice of the apothecary drifted through her memories.

Marie slammed her hands down on the table, shaking the contents. "I will not stop until I can destroy her. But I need more, I need to be stronger, you didn't see what she's capable of."

"And how many will you create to satisfy this need? Every failed attempt dooms another soul. You are becoming what you hate. You are no better than she is, I will have no further part in this blasphemy." The apothecary walked away and began to clean the workspace.

"Forgive me friend. All this time you have been an ally, but you are correct, I am changing, these people we have taken, they were innocent. They did not deserve the path that I chose for them. I wish to try one more time, only this time, the test subject shall be me."

The apothecary sighed heavily, he walked to the back of his shop, moving some boxes and scrolls, revealing a small door in the wall. He opened the lock and removed a small piece of parchment, it was only a scrap from a larger piece, Marie wondered at the significance of it.

"I do know what she is capable of, I have seen her kind destroy my village, only a few of us were able to escape. I have lived with that horror all my life. This parchment was taken from what we called the Tome of the Damned. It chronicled every supernatural creature ever to exist, how they were created and how to destroy them. For years I tried, as we have, to create a way to destroy them all, but I failed. But perhaps you will see the way." He handed the scrap to Marie.

"You've had this all this time and never said anything?" She asked confused.

"When you came here you were lost and confused but still pure of heart. Now we have both lost our way. I only pray we can find it again."

Marie looked at the small vial, almost empty of the valuable blood, she only had this one chance. For days she neither slept nor ate as she poured over the scrap, portions were in a language foreign to her. They struggled to translate it, but nothing made sense, there was no answer to be found.

Marie laid her head down on the table, exhausted, allowing sleep to claim her. The bell dinged, signaling the arrival of a customer. It was Widow Caddel.

"Ah child, I'm out of my unguent for my pains, could you be a dear and make me some?"

Marie hurried to gather her items and make a space for the work, the scrap of parchment fluttering out of her hands, landing in front of the widow. "Bringer of the Dawn? What foolishness are you reading girl?"

"Dawn? Forgive me but I believe it says Death..."

"No girl, my grandmother spoke this language and taught me well, death would have a different shape here and here, this word is dawn."

Marie and the apothecary looked at each other, could it have been so simple as a mistaken word? Marie quickly made the unguent and hurried the widow on her way, the old woman protesting all the while the younger woman was guiding her to the door.

Marie and the apothecary looked at the passage again, the meaning completely different with the change of wording.

"Tonight we create a new potion, then it must catch the

rays of the Dawn, you must drink it as the Full Moon rises."

Marie nodded and spent the day preparing for their final attempt. As the sun rose, they watched the vial sitting in the window, it bubbled and smoked, then the color changed from black to gold and everything was silent.

Marie took the vial from the window and held it for the apothecaries inspection. "All we can do now is wait."

As night fell and the full moon rose, Marie stepped out the back door of the building, into the small courtyard beyond. She was free from prying eyes. With a small prayer for salvation, Marie opened the vial, drank the contents and the burning began.

Beep, beep, beep. The constant noise finally woke Marie from her dream. She could smell the antiseptic scent of the hospital. "Damn." She thought to herself, this was not where she wanted to be.

"I'm sorry officer, you are incorrect," she heard from beyond the door, "there is no evidence that the young woman was shot, she barely has any damage at all."

"No! I was there. I saw her get shot!" The officer argued back.

"The only thing odd about this woman is her blood, my sample must have been contaminated because it is not normal."

"Crap, they have my blood." After all these centuries, one would think she would have done better on the first meeting, but it seemed she was rusty. She needed to get out of here and destroy those samples.

Marie grabbed the IV needle, yanked it from her arm, then removed the other monitoring devices causing an alarm to blare. The officer stepped into the room.

"Hey take it easy. You need to rest."

"No, I need to leave."

"How did you heal like that? I saw you get shot."

"No Mark, you were mistaken." Marie felt dirty as she compelled him to believe her lie. She hated this 'gift' but it was necessary now. "Go home, forget this night."

The officer walked out of the room in a daze as Marie yanked the power cord from the wall, silencing the monitor, someone would be there soon to check on her. She slipped into the hall, still in her hospital gown, she ducked into the room next door, the occupant was asleep but her clothes were safely bundled in the bag next to the bed.

Marie took the top and pants, which were a little too big, quickly changed and walked from the room, closing the door behind her. She scanned the hospital map, looking for the lab, then walked that way. She found a doctor scanning his badge and quickly caught the door before it closed.

"Miss, I'm sorry, you cannot be in here." The doctor said as he noticed her, then his eyes widened as he recognized her. "You? How did you get here?"

"I'm sorry, I can't let you study me anymore. You will go home, you will forget I, and my blood, ever existed."

The doctor left the room in a daze, Marie looked at the computer screen, she prayed he hadn't shared this with anyone. She wiped the computer memory, then noticed her baton on a side table.

"Burned skin?" Read the note attached to it. She took the baton, noticing a crack in the silver with what looked like parchment inside. Marie walked to the refrigerator housing the blood samples. She was running out of time, she took the samples, smashed them on the ground, then grabbed the flammable chemicals and poured them on top, lighting the puddle and igniting the room. Marie grabbed the doctors coat and mask as she hurried from the room and disappeared down the hall as alarms blared behind her.

CHAPTER SIX

Glass shattered as Lorelai burst through the window of the convenience store a few blocks from the club, the 'Come on in' sign clattering on the floor.

"I think I will." Lorelai growled as she made her way toward the clerk, who screamed as the blood soaked demon made her way forward.

The clerk's husband stepped from the back room with a shotgun, yelling at Lorelai to stay back before firing off two shots into her torso as she continued her path toward his wife. Lorelai sprang toward him before he could reload and sank her fangs into his neck, draining him as his wife cowered in the corner.

"Please, please." She whimpered.

"Oh, don't worry, I won't kill you. I have a better use for you." Lorelai said, as she reached for the cowering woman. "What a lovely outfit." She purred. Lorelai sunk her fangs into the woman's neck, draining her as well before taking off her blood soaked costume and replacing it with the woman's clothing. She then put the costume on the woman, grabbing a pair of scissors from the counter to cut her dark hair into the same short haircut Lorelai currently wore.

Lorelai smiled, then using the scissors, stabbed into her palm, creating a pool of dark blood. She poured a little into the mouth of each of her victims. "Time to have a little fun." She laughed as she shuffled out the back door, her wounds were still healing and she needed rest. Her new creations would throw the Huntress off her scent for a short while, but she knew she could not stay at her apartment to recover.

Lorelai quickly returned to her apartment, stripping it

of anything important, throwing it all into a bag, including the storybook. She considered torching the place, but decided against it. She had had enough of the humans and their police tonight. She crawled out the window and leapt to the ground.

Down the street she could hear the sounds of two people arguing. Lorelai crept along the shadows, the man was trying to get the woman to go with him, but she didn't want to. Lorelai stepped from the shadows, grabbing his arm as it swung toward the woman.

"She said no." Lorelai growled as she grabbed his keys, then threw him into the wall, the cracking sound sickening as he slumped to the ground.

"Thank you so much, you saved my life." The woman threw herself against Lorelai, sobbing uncontrollably.

"You're welcome, little dinner."

"What?" The confused woman looked at her, her relief changing to panic as she saw Lorelai's fangs sparkling in the moonlight as they came toward her.

Lorelai wiped her mouth as she dropped the woman. She was beginning to feel better, but she still needed more. She climbed into the car and drove away.

She couldn't go to the ranch now, the Huntress was too close. She couldn't risk her finding the nest. Where could she go to escape her, yet find victims to wake the others? It was time for them to awaken. She would not be stopped again.

Lorelai continued to drive as the rain began to fall. The passing miles doing nothing for her temper that continued to rage. She would find a way to destroy that creature once and for all, so her kind could rule the Earth as they were always meant to.

As the moon began to set, Lorelai knew she needed to find shelter. Her kind had few weaknesses, but sunlight was unfortunately one of them. As Queen, she could withstand it more than most, but in her weakened state, she was not interested in the burning she knew she would feel.

Ahead, she saw the blazing lights of a house. As she drew

closer, she saw the house had strange old lettering on it. Perfect, she thought to herself as she pulled in front of the frat house.

She walked to the door and rang the doorbell. A large, beefy man answered, Lorelai assumed human females would find him attractive, but she only saw him as breakfast.

"Please, my car broke down," Lorelai lied, fluttering her eyelashes, pushing up her bosom, "please help me. May I come in?"

The man looked her up and down, obviously under the influence of whatever he had been drinking that night. He focused on her heaving bosom before standing aside and letting her in, the door closing softly behind them.

CHAPTER SEVEN

Marie locked the door of the seedy motel room, twitching the curtains slightly as she peeked out the window. She didn't think she'd been followed, but she couldn't let her guard down now that Lorelai knew she was close. The stay in the hospital had been too much of a risk. It was time to move on, she was so close to Lorelai, possibly even the nest, but she couldn't risk being discovered.

As time passed and technology advanced, it made Marie's existence so much harder to hide. She could no longer just move from town to town or country to country, she needed passports, identification, and various identifying numbers. These could be difficult to attain and even harder to know who to trust in her quest to obtain the documents.

Marie sat on the edge of the bed, she wearily rubbed her face. She was tired, so very tired. Tired of this existence, tired of this eternal chase. She needed to find a way to end it all, so she could finally rest.

Her eyes came to rest on her baton, laying on the bedside table. The crack in the metal shimmered softly in the glow of the lamp. Her heart ached as she bent the baton, exposing the parchment inside. This weapon was the final piece she had from her grandmother, now it was ruined. She would need to find a way to create something to fight Lorelai, but everything she had tried had failed, only her grandmother's weapons could hurt the monster.

With shaking hands she removed the fragile sheet. Her breath caught as she recognized her grandmothers bold script.

'To my dearest granddaughter,

I can only hope that you find this in
my lifetime, though in my heart
I know you may not. You are the last
of our line, the only hope for
destroying evil once and for all.
For centuries, our family has hunted
the descendants of the first vampire Ambrogio
and his beloved Selene.'

Marie stopped reading, Ambrogio? She had never heard of this vampire. How had she not known of the first vampire? She continued reading.

'Our ancestor was a maiden of the temple
for the Oracle at Delphi. She was a witness
to the creation of Ambrogio, she carefully
wrote down everything that had happened
and how to destroy him and his kind.
Unfortunately, his beloved Selene
discovered her and what she believed
to be treachery. Selene destroyed her
scrolls after our ancestor fled the temple.
Hidden away, she shed her promises to
the temple and started a family.
Teaching her children the dangers
of the vampires and how to destroy
them. Over time her descendants
fought the vampires, continuing to
document their findings. Finally,
one of her ancestors came to reside at
the Serapeum. They convinced the
others to create a great tomb of
knowledge, but they would place it
in the one place the followers of
Ambrogio would never be able to
reach. Selene destroyed any repository

of knowledge, in the hopes that
all truth of their existence would
be lost, but these few scrolls remain.
You must find this tomb
and retrieve this ancient knowledge.
Only then can we ever truly defeat
Lorelai.'

"Serapeum..." Marie muttered to herself. Well she had been in America long enough. It was time to return across the ocean. Marie cast a lingering glance at the bed, wishing she could rest, but she knew the longer she stayed there, the more time Lorelai had to gain strength and followers.

Taking her few possessions, she slipped out of the room and past the front office. Through the window she could see the television flickering, showing the hospital and a fuzzy picture of herself as a person of interest.

"Damn." She muttered to herself as she hurried down the street. Now was definitely the time to change personas and leave the country. She grabbed a hoodie from an outside vendor, quietly leaving a twenty on the register while the owners back was turned.

Marie pulled the hood up over her face and continued on toward the bus station. It was so cliché but she had dozens of lockers, all over the world with money and identification. It was never much, but it was enough to buy tickets to wherever she needed to go.

She didn't even need to look in the locker to know which identity she needed. The small backpack contained everything she needed to change into her new persona. Marie slowly walked to the restroom at the farthest end of the station. Locking herself into the stall, she opened the backpack and let out a sigh. She hated this part.

Marie pulled out the box of hair dye and the scissors. She quickly cut her hair to the shoulder length style in the passport photo and applied the bleach. Her foot wiggled on the floor as she stood in the stall, waiting for the bleach to work.

A knock resounded on the door. "Still busy." Marie responded as the woman moved to another stall. She knew the odor from the box dye was noticeable, she pulled a small bottle of perfume from the backpack and sprayed a few sprays into the air.

"Damn druggies." She could hear the woman mutter as she did her business and left the bathroom. When the room was silent, Marie left the stall and blocked the main door. Then she quickly rinsed her hair and dried it as best she could using towels and the air dryer.

She ran her fingers through her new hairstyle, then shoved the hoodie and pants into the backpack with the box from the hair dye. She looked at her reflection, with her smart business suit and professional hair style, she now looked every bit the part of her next character, Dr. Allison Mattingly, Archaeologist.

CHAPTER EIGHT

"Welcome aboard and enjoy your flight Dr. Mattingly." Said the ticket agent with a smile, as she handed the ticket and passport back to Marie. Marie watched as her new suitcase disappeared into the back to be loaded on to the plane.

She had taken a little extra time to shop, so she could buy the suitcase and a few additional outfits prior to her trip. She didn't want to look strange traveling overseas with no luggage. Even the one small suitcase had received a strange look from the ticket agent, but a stern look from 'Dr. Mattingly' had changed her attitude.

Marie clutched her shoulder bag and walked to the first class lounge. She still had a small wait before boarding, she had purchased a tablet to do some research. Marie sat in the corner of the lounge with a steaming cup of tea and unpacked the tablet.

"New tablet eh?" Came a voice behind her. "You really should have set that up before the flight."

"Yes," she laughed, "my old one just died and it had everything on it. I'm hoping I can retrieve it all." Marie really wasn't in the mood for a conversation, but the man was soon sitting next to her, looking at the tablet.

"Let me help you with that. I'm pretty good with these things."

"Oh, no thank you. I uploaded everything to the sky."

"The sky? You mean the cloud? You definitely need my help."

Marie cursed to herself. She would never remember all these new terms. History she knew, she had lived it, but technology was not her forte.

"Flight 602 to Dubai now boarding at Gate 2."

Marie placed her tablet in her shoulder bag and stood. "Thank you but my flight is boarding."

"You are traveling to Dubai as well? Perhaps you will allow me to show you some of my city."

"I only have a brief layover before I continue on to my next destination. Thank you for the offer but I am on a tight schedule." Marie walked toward the gate, her new companion close beside, attempting to make conversation.

"This way Dr. Mattingly." The flight attendant smiled as she gestured toward first class.

"Thank you for the conversation sir, but this is where we part I'm afraid."

"Ah Dr. Ashref, a pleasure as always. Your regular seat is waiting." Dr. Ashref gave a slight bow to Marie and settled into his seat. Marie gave a brief smile and found her seat, pulling the tablet from her bag, waiting until the flight attendant gave the all clear for electronics.

Soon the plane was in the air and the ground gave way to the waves below. Marie booted up the tablet and logged in, quickly doing any searches she could on Selene and Ambrogio. There was mention of a titan goddess named Selene who resided in the Temple of Delphi and a brief mention of an Italian named Ambrogio but nothing extraordinary. It was like the story had been wiped from existence.

Marie felt a movement next to her and looked up into the chocolate eyes of Dr. Ashref. "Please forgive my rudeness earlier. I only meant to assist you but it appears I was mistaken."

Marie sighed and put her tablet down. "You have no reason to be forgiven. The fault was my own. I sometimes forget how to interact with others. I was doing some research and was focused on that. Though it seems I am at a dead end for the moment."

Dr. Ashref gestured to the empty seat next to Marie. "May I join you then? Perhaps I can assist you in your journey for knowledge."

"Please sit, though perhaps we can just chat. A break might just be what I need."

"Thank you, Dr. Mattingly was it? I am Dalil Ashref."

"Allison." Marie replied extending her hand. "You are a Dr. as well?"

"Ah yes, I have a small research house in Dubai. It is not well known but I tend to travel much to share my findings. You said you travel through Dubai to another destination?"

"Yes, I am an Archaeologist. I'm headed to Alexandria and the soonest flight was with a layover in Dubai."

"Then I'm glad that the gods allowed our paths to cross. I am pleased to meet you Allison."

Marie smiled at the older gentleman. It had been many years since a human had put her at such ease. The rest of the flight they engaged in small talk between meals and rest. Too soon, the pilot was announcing their arrival in Dubai and Marie knew it was time to focus on the task at hand.

Dr. Ashref handed her a card as he said his goodbyes. "If you ever need anything, please do not hesitate to call." With a brief bow, he disappeared into the crowd, and Marie was once again alone.

The layover was dull as Marie continued to scroll through the pages of the internet. Every page less helpful than the last. Finally in frustration, she turned off the tablet and shoved it into her bag. Perhaps she should change her ticket and travel to Greece, to the ruins of Delphi?

The overhead announcement called for the boarding of her next flight and Marie headed toward the gate. She had already called ahead and she had colleagues waiting for this flight to arrive. She would cause a commotion if she did not arrive on time. Perhaps after Alexandria she could travel to Greece.

Marie napped sporadically on the brief flight to Alexandria, then quickly found her name on the signs held by the drivers as she left the airport. Waiting in the car was her longtime colleague and friend, Dr. Roger Blackbourn. He was one of the few people she trusted with her true identity.

"The Serapeum?" He said in his proper English accent. "What are you searching for there? It was raided centuries ago, there simply isn't anything left." Marie pulled the parchment from her bag and handed it to him. "Ahh, I see. Well, it is too late to go now. Perhaps dinner, then to the hotel. At first light we will see what we can find."

Marie nodded and looked out the window. The city sped by the window, lights beginning to shine as the sun disappeared below the horizon. As per his usual, dinner was at the fanciest restaurant in town. They kept the conversation casual, one never knew who was listening.

They made arrangements to meet for breakfast before first light and he walked her to her hotel room. "It is always a pleasure to see you my dear. I hope we can solve your mystery this time."

As Marie sat in the room, sleep escaped her. She returned again and again to the tablet. The partial stories of the Oracle and Ambrogio pulling her in. She knew this was a part of the tale that she needed to unravel. Her grandmother had mentioned the name, there had to be more.

The phone next to her head rang, waking her from her slumber. She had fallen asleep, hunched over the desk, her tablet still glowing in the dark.

"Are we still having breakfast?" Roger asked confused.

"Yes, sorry, I will be right down." Marie dressed quickly in her field clothes and hurried downstairs. As she entered the room, Roger and another man turned to face her. "Dr. Ashref."

CHAPTER NINE

"A pleasure to see you again, Dr. Mattingly." Dr. Ashref stepped forward and greeted Marie. "Please forgive the intrusion, Dr. Blackbourn called me late last evening and asked if I could help on your quest. He felt I may have some insight into your mystery."

Marie paled, had she been betrayed? What had Roger told him? She glanced nervously at Roger, he shook his head almost imperceptively. Marie let out a small sigh of relief, she should have known Roger would only tell what was needed.

"How do you feel you can assist us, Dr.? What exactly is your realm of expertise?"

Dr. Ashref chuckled, his friendly face animated. "I study mythos, I search to see the reality behind the fantasy. Every myth comes from some form of reality, no matter how small."

"And you feel this would be helpful to me how?"

"You seek the ancient Tomb of the Serapeum. Few have heard the myth, fewer still know of its actual existence."

"And you are one of these few?"

"I am." A smile lit his face as he spoke. "I feel we should discuss this matter in a more private setting. The revelation of the existence of this tomb would cause a massive uproar in the black market community. The legends of the treasures contained within the tomb are immense."

"I only wish to find a scroll."

"Only a scroll? What could be on a scroll that would be of such interest? It is said that the journey to the tomb is deadly to all but those who have the secret key."

"Then we will find the key, and you will find, sir, that

I am very difficult to kill." Marie stepped out the door of the small restaurant and hailed a cab. "Shall we travel to the ruins gentlemen?"

The three companions traveled to the ruins of the Serapeum in silence, Marie running through the note from her grandmother in her mind. What was she looking for? What was the key? Did Dr. Ashref know the location or was he just another dead end?

The cab pulled up to the ruins and Roger paid him, signaling for the cabbie to leave them and return in a few hours time. "You see? The site has been plundered, there isn't anything here."

"There has to be something. The parchment said the Tomb was beyond where they could reach it. Perhaps its not on land?" Marie looked toward the ocean. Vampires could not touch the water... perhaps the tomb was in the bay?

"What parchment? Who can't reach it?" Dr. Ashref questioned.

"I came into possession of a piece of parchment giving a brief description of the location, but nothing concrete."

"May I see the parchment?"

"I... I don't have it with me."

"Perhaps later then." Dr. Ashref said sadly.

"Perhaps."

Dr. Blackbourn looked thoughtful for a moment, then replied. "You may have something, Allison. Underwater would make it difficult for anyone of the time to reach. But where could it be that it has not been discovered yet? And how can we reach it and get inside?"

"According to my research," Dr. Ashref began, "there will be a series of tests in order to reach the tomb. It would seem we need to create a bond of trust between us. As I am the newest to this group, I will go first."

He pulled a tablet from his bag, pushing the button, the screen illuminating quickly, showing scans of an ancient text. "According to this text, the Tomb was created sometime after the reign of Ptolemy III Euergetes. It was created to house the greatest and most valuable knowledge, and keep it safe from an unnamed destructive force. Not long after the completion and hiding of the Tomb, the Great Library was destroyed. Many attribute this to Alexander the Great, but this text claims that a woman of great evil came to the city first, she destroyed all knowledge, both written and human alike."

Marie and Roger exchanged a glance. How much could they tell the doctor without revealing her secret?

"The first clue is hidden here in these ruins," he continued, showing them a picture of a stone with a hole in it, "I have never been able to open the lock, but I know where to begin."

"Show me." Marie stated bluntly.

Dr. Ashref led the way through the ruins to a small, unassuming stone in the center. The weather beaten stone had a small hole in it, as well as an aged symbol that Marie could barely make out. A symbol she had seen every day of her life. The symbol of her family.

"Allison..." Roger began.

"I know." She reached into her bag and retrieved the broken baton, removing the wooden spike on one end. Revealing the symbol underneath, the same as the one on the stone. She heard a sharp intake of breath behind her.

"You have the key." Dr. Ashref whispered in awe.

Marie inserted the baton into the hole and turned. Nothing. She tried again. Still nothing.

"Perhaps when it broke, it destroyed the key." She said sadly.

"May I?" Dr. Ashref asked, holding out his hand. Marie handed him the broken baton and he examined it. Then he grasped the end and twisted it sharply, the end opened to reveal multiple prongs. "Try it now."

Marie looked at him confused but took the baton and tried again. This time there was a click and a rumble, and a door opened in the rock revealing an inscription written in ancient

Greek.

"Go back to where it all began." They all read aloud.

"Where it began? But the Tomb was created here. Where would we go?"

"Delphi... We need to find the Oracle of Delphi."

CHAPTER TEN

Lorelai let the body slip through her fingers and down to the floor. "Clean that up." She ordered the man standing next to her, who was staring straight ahead, avoiding looking at his dead frat brother.

"Yes, my Queen." He responded, grabbing the limp body, dragging it from the room. Lorelai smirked and wiped her lips. In the short time she had been staying at the house, she had brought all of them under her power. She really shouldn't have killed the boy, but she was so hungry and he tasted so good.

Her new minions had held a special Rush event, to recruit new members, more sacrifices for her. Why had she never thought of this before? The boys had done everything for her. The young pledges were either used by her as food, or enthralled to save for later as sacrifices to wake the others.

She sighed, pleased with herself for her progress, but she knew she couldn't stay here much longer. The few that she had actually killed would be missed and someone would come looking. She couldn't get too confident. She needed to keep her plans quiet until she woke the others, then they could feed. The streets would run red.

The man returned from his grizzly chore, she didn't know what he had done with the body, nor did she care. She knew her little minion was very adept at hiding her leftovers. Such a pity he was only human.

The television blared in the other room, left unnoticed as others had gone about their day. "No leads on the hospital fire, police are still looking for this woman." The reporter said, smiling into the camera.

If only Lorelai had a clue as to where Marie had disappeared to, she could alert the police and keep her away a while longer. But she had seen no evidence that Marie was close. The last she had seen of her since their fight was the news footage of the hospital burning with the grainy photo of her walking from the building.

Lorelai knew it was her, they had hunted each other so long she knew every inch of that woman. She could never create a disguise that would fool her. Maybe it was the small amount of blood Marie had used to create the vile potion that allowed her to live on, that created that small link between them.

"My Queen? Is there anything you require?" Came the soft voice from behind her. He wanted her, she knew it and it made her want to wretch. Humans! Yuck, the thought of mating with him disgusted her. He was only a minion, slightly more important than food to her.

"Yes, my pet. We are going on a trip. Tell your brothers to get ready, we will leave within the hour."

"Where are we going, my Queen?" He questioned.

"To my home, of course, where you will all be rewarded for your loyalty." She gave him a sly smile, then shooed him off to complete his task. Lorelai watched the moon rise as the others loaded bags into their vehicles to prepare for the road trip. They wouldn't need what was in the bags, but she didn't dissuade them from taking them. Best not to cause alarm. "Yes, do dress nicely. We do want you all to make a good impression."

Lorelai climbed into the car, enjoying an uneventful ride to the quiet, unassuming ranch. The entire ride basking in the glow of her first bit of success. These sacrifices would wake many of the most important members of her coven.

Once they were awakened, they would gather more of their human cattle, feasting until the entire nest was awakened, then they would finally rule over this world, as it was always meant to be. She had allowed the population to overtake the capacity of the Earth. They would never want for food, her children would never feel the crushing thirst ever again.

The car came to a stop in front of the farmhouse, light spilled from the windows and open door, giving the illusion of welcome and safety. In the doorway stood her gatekeeper, his eyes glittered as they roved over the group of men assembling in front of the house.

"Please show them into the guest room, they are all here to meet my family." Lorelai instructed him. "Do make sure they are comfortable." He bowed as he held the door open for the group.

"As you wish, my lady."

Lorelai grabbed the arm of her most faithful minion. "Except for you, my pet. I wish for you to accompany me... alone."

The man gulped as he looked into her eyes, his heart racing. They had never been truly alone. Perhaps she finally would give him what he desired.

Lorelai opened the secret staircase and began to descend. The man followed, an icy chill running up his spine. Lorelai looked back and smiled. "Do not worry my pet. Do you not trust me?"

He became at ease, following her into the depths of the nest. When they reached the bottom of the staircase, Lorelai grabbed a torch from a holder, walking down one of the side tunnels. She stopped in front of one of the doors and opened it.

"In here," she gestured for him to follow her, "you will get everything you deserve." They walked into the dark room, in the center was some sort of raised stone bench. Lorelai pushed him down on top, she could feel his pulse racing. He was excited, poor boy.

She grabbed his arm and took a small dagger from her belt. She slit his arm, watching the blood run down on to the bench.

"My Queen?" He said confused. "What are you doing?"

"My pure little pet, you have let no woman touch you, let no drug enter your body, no alcohol pass your lips. You are as pure as a newborn." She cooed to him, as she watched the blood run in a stream into a small channel cut into the bench. She squeezed his arm ever so slightly, allowing the blood to flow more from the cut.

"I am only for you." He breathed, his eyes hooded as he leaned forward to kiss her.

"Oh no, my pet. You were never for me." She smiled as she watched the blood drain into a hole in the bench. She pushed him back against the stone again as she held the torch higher. He realized in horror that he lay on no bench. He was laying on a coffin. A deep growl came from beneath him and the stone began to shake.

"My Queen." He pleaded, full of fear. "Have I not been faithful? Have I not done everything you asked of me without question? Do you not care for me?"

Lorelai laughed harshly. "Care for you? Yes, my pet. I care for you as a farmer cares for his stock. I have tended you as my prize steer, my pure one, to give strength to the most important member of my coven."

Lorelai stepped back as the stone shook, then shattered, throwing the man to the ground in the destruction.

"My Queen, please. Please." His voice rose in desperation. "Nooooooo."

CHAPTER ELEVEN

1153 AD

"Help! Please help me." The hooded woman cried out as she ran through the darkened village, stumbling as she ran. She looked back in terror as the shadowy figure advanced on her through the darkness, its weapons glistening in the moonlight. "Help, please!" She cried out again, her voice shrill with desperation.

Ahead a door opened, the soft light of a candle filled the doorway. The woman tripped and fell at the butchers feet with a small thud. As she looked up into his eyes with her tear streaked face, her hood fell back, revealing her dark hair and pale face.

"Save me, please. She means to kill me, she said she wants my heart." Sobs wracked Lorelai's body as she continued her charade for the man. Blood dripped down her arm, evidence of a struggle.

"Nikolai, get away from her. She's dangerous." Marie called out, hurrying from the shadows. Lorelai looked deep into the butchers eyes, pulling him under her spell. He stepped from the doorway, placing himself between the two women. Soft sobs still could be heard from the woman lying prone on the ground.

Nikolai looked at the weapons in Marie's hands, blood evident on the tip of one. "It would seem, madam, that you are the only dangerous creature here. Be gone, or I will call the guards."

"Nikolai, you have known me all these years. I would never hurt anyone, but she is dangerous, she needs to be stopped."

A crowd had started to gather now. "I've seen her attack children. She eats their hearts." A small man called from the back of the crowd, his eyes glittering evilly.

"Yes, I've seen her too." His brother called. "She did something horrible to Old Thomas. Remember we found him mutilated last week? Drive her from the town. Stone her." He reached down, grabbed a stone and threw it at her, hitting her in the shoulder.

"No, she has you under her spell. She will kill you all." Marie backed away, dodging more and more stones as the street filled with angry villagers. It became a mob as more of her neighbors turned on her, fueled by the rage of the enthralled villagers.

Torches and pitchforks soon were brought to the front of the crowd, Marie faced people she thought of as friends, staring at her in hatred. Behind the crowd, Lorelai and her minion stared at her, all pretenses of fear and crying wiped away. Lorelai smirked as the butcher stepped forward.

"You will leave this town and never return. If we ever see a hair from your head, your life is forfeit. You thought you could come to our village, you could rule our people and tell them what to do. Well, we will protect our own... and you, evil creature, no longer have power over any of us."

"Nikolai," Marie said, a tear slipping down her cheek, "I would never do any of those things, and I promise to protect you all as best I can."

"Don't listen to her. She tried to kill me." Lorelai whimpered.

Nikolai glared at Marie. "We don't want your protection, we don't need your protection."

The crowd riled again as Lorelai's minion called for her death. Marie turned sadly from the only place she had called home since she had destroyed her own. Blood ran down her temple as another stone hit her.

Out of the corner of her eye, she saw the apothecary standing in his doorway, a sad expression on his face. Marie shook her head slightly at him to let him know he could not interfere and slipped into the darkness.

"Come, my lady, please come into my house. You will be safe here." Nikolai put an arm around Lorelai and led her into his house. Her minions followed, their eyes glittering with hunger.

* * * *

Lorelai sighed softly as she sat back on the soft bed and closed the storybook. Once she had created the scene in the village, it had been so easy to bend and stretch the tale. Embellishing it over time, making it flourish, until one day it was written into a book, some many versions of her wonderful lie.

Lorelai rose and returned to the lower levels of the nest. The screams had finally ceased, many of her followers had been awakened.

"We live to serve." Nikolai kneeled before her. Blood still fresh on his lips.

"Rise, my hunter, rise and gather more so we may waken the others. The time has finally come for us to rule this world. Tonight we feast!"

Laughter filled the room as they all rushed up the stairs and into the night. There was no way to stop them now. She thought as her lips curled in triumph.

CHAPTER TWELVE

Roger handed Marie an envelope. "Two tickets to Athens. It may not be the closest airport to Delphi, but it was the only one I could get tickets to on such short notice. There will be a car waiting when you arrive."

"Two?" Marie questioned. "You will not be coming?"

"Forgive me, though the mystery is interesting, I still have a job to do. The university would not take kindly to me disappearing for days. Besides I need to set up a way for you to locate, and get to the Tomb. If we work on this problem from multiple angles, we will work faster."

"Work smarter, not harder?" Marie replied wryly.

"Spot on." Roger smiled. He longed for the adventure, but he had responsibilities, he couldn't draw extra attention to Marie's quest by going with her. There would be explanations to give and they didn't have the time to make them. "The clue doesn't give much information, who knows how many more clues there will be. Be safe, trust no one and return with the answer."

Marie laughed. "You make it sound so easy. As you say though, we don't know anything except to go to Delphi, though even that is just a hunch based on grandmother's stories. I will trust Dr. Ashref because I trust you, but aside from that we will keep to ourselves."

Roger nodded and gave Marie an awkward hug. "Time to go save the world, my dear."

Marie walked away, for the first time in a long time she was nervous. Lorelai had grown stronger in her years of rest. She had hidden her nest well, Marie knew why she had bided her time, she knew Lorelai encouraged humanity to flourish like a farmer tending his stock, and she knew that the population had gotten to a point that it could sustain a large amount of vampires with no problems.

Lorelai had played an intelligent waiting game. She knew what her kind needed to survive but she also knew what they needed to flourish. She had been different in their last meeting, almost desperate to be rid of Marie. The time was coming for their final battle and if Marie failed, humanity was lost.

Marie climbed into the car, staring out the window, lost in thought. It all came down to this, all the searching and training. The waiting and wondering. Everything led to this moment, and it all balanced on her ability to follow some ancient clues to determine what her ancestors had left behind.

They arrived at the airport and hurried to their plane. Roger hadn't left them much time to dawdle as the call for boarding echoed over the loud speaker as they arrived.

The plane trip was as uneventful as the car ride. Marie could hear the drone of people talking around her. She could hear Dr. Ashref attempt to pull her into conversation a few times, but she was lost in her thoughts. Remembering every meeting she had with Lorelai over the years, from the murder of her family, to the fight in the street Halloween night. She dredged through every memory of lore she had read, anything she had found that spoke of Lorelai. She thought back to her childhood and replayed every story her grandmother had told her, before she even knew that vampires truly existed.

Soon came the announcement that they would be landing, and Marie pulled herself out of her thoughts. Dr. Ashref smiled in understanding as she looked at him, ready to begin the search and answer the questions.

An unassuming grey sedan was waiting for them. After they gathered their small amount of luggage, they drove north. It was a few hours drive to the temple. Roger had made them a reservation at one of the local hotels, they checked in quickly before heading to the temple. The ruins glistened in the setting sun.

"I would assume what we are looking for will have the same marking as the stone in Alexandria. Probably somewhere out of sight." Dr. Ashref muttered to himself.

Marie walked to the guard, handing him a letter from Roger. "I believe you're expecting us? We're here to do some research on the ruins."

"Yes, Dr. Blackbourn phoned ahead. Drs. Mattingly and Ashref?" They both pulled out their ID's as the guard walked them into the site. "We close at sunset, for your safety you will have to leave at that time." They nodded as they walked past the fence.

Marie walked to the center of the ruins, to the spot the Oracle herself would have sat to have her visions. She turned around looking at the ruins.

"What are you looking for?" Dr. Ashref questioned.

"The chambers of the maidens. Everything started here, in the Temple of Apollo, my ancestor was one of the maidens of the Temple. If it started here, it started with her."

"I believe the chambers would be this way, there were many maidens who served the temple. This could take a while." They started forward to begin their search for the chambers.

"I'm sorry, we're closing now. Please make your way to the parking lot." The guard said from behind them. Dr. Ashref gestured to Marie. "My dear? Let's return to the hotel for dinner."

"We cannot wait. We have to come back tonight." Marie hissed as they walked away.

"I understand your rush, but if we search in the dark, we could easily miss it or get caught by the guard seeing our flashlight. I propose we rest, then return at opening tomorrow, we will have the day to search without looking suspicious then we can return after closing to explore whatever we find."

Marie sighed, he was right, she was rushing in her need to stop Lorelai, almost as if the Vampire Queen's desperation had infected her. Her stomach rumbled as she responded. "I agree, it's foolhardy to not be careful in our investigation. We must find the way to enter the Tomb, but we cannot be hasty."

The next morning, Marie and Dr. Ashref were up before the sun rose, waiting for the site to open.

"Ah good morning Drs., back again I see." The guard smiled as he invited them in. Dr. Ashref tipped his hat as he walked by the guard.

They wandered through the ruins, searching every inch of wall and column. It all looked the same, broken and weathered. The sun moved past its zenith, yet still they searched. Dr. Ashref pulled two sack lunches from his backpack, as they ate their eyes continued to rove over the stones.

As the sun dipped toward the horizon, they moved to the farthest part of the ruins, there was what appeared to have been a small room. Marie entered the space, more of the same. She turned to leave, noticing a change in the wall between the door and the corner. She walked out the door, it was different than the others. It was almost imperceptible but it was there.

She called to Dr. Ashref. "Look at this wall, it's different than the others."

"Yes, someone skilled has changed the wall." They entered the small room again and looked carefully at the wall. The wall ran smoothly to the corner, only the fine lines of the stones showing. Dr. Ashref hurried from the room to the other side of the wall.

"Dr. Mattingly, I've found it." Marie hurried to find him. There in the corner of the adjoining room, hidden in the shadow of the corner was a small hole marked with her ancestors seal.

CHAPTER THIRTEEN

1410 BC

Ohanna walked into the main chamber, a fresh bowl of fruit in her hands, an offering to Apollo.
She had only recently arrived at the temple, a great honor bestowed upon her and her family. The other maidens of the temple were busy with their tasks as well. Selene stood behind her sister, Pythia, the Oracle, a wife of their God Apollo. Selene was always there to attend her sister, she was a favorite among the temple maidens.

It was said that Selene was a goddess as well, but rumor did not matter to Ohanna, they were all sisters now, there to worship Apollo, to assure that those who came for his guidance, through the Oracle, were seen. Ohanna placed the bowl of fruit on the table and turned to leave. She noticed a man coming down the stairs into the room. She stepped back to wait and see if Selene would need anything for the vision.

Ohanna waited quietly, hands clasped, her eyes down as the Oracle moved to her tripod seat over the cracks in the floor. She had never witnessed the Oracle give a vision before. The man still had blood on his hands from the sacrifice he had made at the altar outside. Ohanna could see Selene whispering into the Oracle's ear as she began to wash her sister with water from the Castalian spring that flowed into the temple.

The Oracle gently nodded her head and held her hand out for her bowl. Selene glanced at Ohanna, Ohanna noticed the bowl on the table next to her. She walked respectfully to Selene with the bowl, keeping her eyes down, again as a sign of respect to the Oracle. Out of the corner of her eye, she saw the older woman smile softly.

Selene filled the bowl with water, then held it out to her sister, who drank the liquid, she settled herself in her chair and breathed deep. Selene handed her a branch of bay laurel. Ohanna hurried quietly back to her spot by the table, she replaced the bowl, then waited, almost holding her breath in anticipation.

The Oracle's head snapped back, her eyes glassy. Her voice came low and not her own. "The curse. The moon. The blood will run." She sank back against Selene, for a brief moment Ohanna could see stark fear in her eyes before she closed them and relaxed against her sister.

"Please, my lady, I do not understand." The man whispered, dropping to his knees in front of the Oracle. Selene caught Ohanna's eye and nodded. Ohanna stepped forward.

"It is time for the Oracle to rest now. She is spent from her visions."

The man nodded, walking with Ohanna to the stairs, his face clouded with deep thought. Ohanna watched him from the corner of her eye, something troubled her about this man. She had never heard a prophecy before, but this one was dark. Was this man a danger? She watched as he walked out the door, then seated himself in the courtyard beyond. Ohanna shrugged, returning to her duties, focusing on the other pilgrims who had traveled to see the Oracle.

The next morning, Ohanna glanced out the window as she rose, she noticed the strange man walking from the courtyard. It was not odd for a traveler to sleep outside the temple, so she put all thoughts of the odd man and his prophecy out of her mind, then left to begin her chores.

Some time later, Selene entered the temple, her cheeks flushed, a soft smile on her face. Ohanna attributed the flush to the morning air, but as the days went on, Selene grew more and more giddy. Secret smiles, humming when she thought she was alone. Ohanna was curious.

The next morning, Ohanna rose early and followed Selene as she went into the town. She wandered around the market, gathering the items they needed for the temple. Ohanna thought perhaps she had been mistaken to doubt Selene, after all she was the sister of the Oracle and a goddess in her own right, who was Ohanna to doubt her?

As she turned to hurry back to the temple, Ohanna caught a glimpse of the strange man. He walked by the booth that Selene was at, then appeared to signal to her. Selene followed him a short time later, Ohanna didn't know what to do. The maidens of the temple were never supposed to be alone with a man, but Selene was her superior.

Ohanna snuck after them, as she peeked around the corner, she caught them in a passionate kiss. Ohanna slammed her back to the wall, hot tears forming. Selene was denying her vows to Apollo. Ohanna's feet flew along the ground, as if the sandals of Hermes were on them. She ran to her cot and laid down, sick at the thought of what she had witnessed.

Before long the tears had dried, what was she doing? Her vows were to Apollo, not Selene! Selene could do what she chose, but Ohanna would follow her vows! Ohanna rose, brushed the wrinkles from her dress and left to attend her duties. As she left the room, she ran into Selene, a joyous expression on her face.

"Ohanna, a need you to help me." She gushed. "I am leaving the temple tonight, I met someone. He's asked me to marry him."

"What? I don't understand. You would deny Apollo and leave your sister?"

"Please be happy for me, he is the most wonderful man." Selene replied, her eyes distant.

"Where did you even meet him? Everyone knows of our vows."

"He came from afar." She breathed, her face dreamy. "His name is Ambrogio."

CHAPTER FOURTEEN

"Pardon me, but we will be closing soon. Please make your way to the exit." The guard said from behind Marie, startling her.

"Yes, of course. We will return again tomorrow."

They drove away, out of sight of the temple and turned off the lights. They pulled into a small side road, waiting until they saw the guards truck leave the site.

"Another may come soon." Marie warned.

"I would expect so. Let's be quick." They hurried back to the ruins, the moonlight illuminating their way, the broken section of baton gripped in Marie's hands. Carefully they slipped among the ruins, to the small room again. Marie turned the base of the baton, once again revealing the key pieces. She silently slipped it into the hole and turned, a click and a thump could be heard, then nothing.

"The other room." Marie said, rising and hurrying to the room next door. Lying on the floor, was a piece of masonry, dislodged by the mechanism within the wall. Inside lay a tightly wrapped scroll, encased in a wax of some sort.

"Shall we retire to the hotel? I believe I would like to enjoy a drink as we examine our find."

Marie nodded, curious about the scroll and the odd encasing. They carefully replaced the masonry, locking the mechanism again.

Back at the hotel, the two pondered the wrapped scroll as it lay on the table. "The wax appears to be completely intact, the scroll should be in pristine condition." Dr. Ashref argued.

"Yes, but exposing it to the air will cause it to degrade. It could be destroyed."

"Then we will photograph it, we document everything. The scroll is meant for you, while I agree that archaeologically it is important, we need the information within and I feel that time is of the essence. Am I correct?"

Marie nodded, she hated the thought of possibly losing another piece of her families history. Clearing her mind, she pulled on her gloves, carefully cutting through the wax and linen below, pulling it away from the scroll within. The scroll looked like it had been written yesterday, the words were crisp and bold.

'To my ancestor,
Our family legacy began
with the temple maiden
Ohanna. She discovered
the truth of the vampires
and vowed that our family
would never forget the
secrets to destroying them
once and for all. For
centuries, our family has
hunted their queen, but to
no avail. Those of us who
are left have decided to
place this knowledge in
a repository, in the one
place the vampires can not
reach. To find this repository,
you must follow the path
of Ambrogio.'

Behind the note was the tale of Ambrogio and his descent into becoming the world's first vampire. The pair read through the pages together, Dr. Ashref could periodically be heard commenting on various new bits of knowledge.

“It would seem we have our journey laid out.” Marie said, looking up from her tablet, the map marked with multiple red X’s.

“I will send a message to Dr. Blackbourn to let him know we will be a few more days.”

“Days? Try a week. In the tale, he made multiple stops. We don’t know from this cryptic message if there will be a clue at each spot, or if some will have nothing. We could miss something easily if we assume that there is no clue, simply because we cannot find it.”

“Then we must assume that each spot contains a clue.” Dr. Ashref said with finality. “It’s vital we reach the repository.”

CHAPTER FIFTEEN

1410 BC

Ambrogio watched Selene walk away, his heart light. He had loved her since the moment he had laid eyes on her, now they would be together. He would return to the temple at dusk and wait for her to come to him.

The day passed slowly as Ambrogio watched the sun travel across the sky, it was almost as if Apollo himself slowed its path. As the sun finally reached the horizon, Ambrogio entered the courtyard of the temple, he settled himself behind a tree to wait for his love.

"Ambrogio!" Boomed a voice. "Show yourself!" A glow came from beyond the tree. Ambrogio peeked from behind his hiding spot, he saw a man, radiant as the morning sun, perfect in every way. "You dare come to MY temple, ask favors of MY Oracle, then attempt to steal one of MY maidens? My favorite?"

Ambrogio shook in fear at the booming voice, all thoughts of happiness draining away. "Forgive me, Oh Great Apollo." He cried, falling to his knees before him.

"The damage is done, pitiful human. You have marred what once was pure. For that you shall be punished. For the rest of your mortal life, you shall never again enjoy the warmth of my sun. When it touches your flesh, it shall burn you and cause you agony. To stay in the sun too long shall cause you a horrifying death." Apollo looked at Ambrogio in disdain.

"And what of Selene?" Ambrogio whispered, daring to ask of his love.

Apollo's eyes flashed. "You shall never again speak her name, Selene is a goddess, she is immortal, over time she will forget you." Apollo raised his hand toward Ambrogio, Ambrogio felt a burning in his flesh, he writhed in pain on the ground. When the pain stopped, he saw that Apollo had left.

One last ray of sunlight fell at the edge of the courtyard, Ambrogio crept from the shade of the tree. Could it be true? Was he truly banished from the light? He slowly extended his hand and inched it toward the stream of light. The burning began the instant the light touched his skin. Ambrogio jerked his hand back.

'The curse.' He remembered the Oracle's prophecy. 'The moon.' He looked wryly at the sliver of moon, peeking above the horizon. Now the moon would be the only light he would see. 'The blood will run.' Ambrogio puzzled over this last line, the others made sense now but what of the blood? A sacrifice perhaps? But to who?

Ambrogio waited for his love, but she never came. The temple was silent. As he waited, he thought about what Apollo had said. 'Selene is immortal... she will forget you.' It was true, even if they had a brief life together, he would die and she would live on. He knew where he must go... Hades.

Ambrogio traveled to the River Acheron, which ran to the gates of the Underworld. The trip took longer than he had anticipated, as he had to find protection during the day. Traveling at night was not as easy as he thought it would be. He had to avoid bandits and pitfalls in the road, multiple times he tripped on various dangers that he would have seen in the light.

Finally he arrived at the cavern that led to the Underworld. He took a deep breath, attempting to calm the nerves in his stomach. If Hades did not accept his bargain, he would be trapped in the Underworld forever. Deeper he went into the cavern, all light seemed to be extinguished, he felt along the wall, stumbling and praying he didn't lose his way.

The tunnel he followed opened at last and a great cavern appeared, illuminated by some unknown source. Ambrogio cowered back, afraid to burn himself again. He gathered his courage, slowly he inched forward into the grey light. He felt no pain, this was not the light of Apollo. He breathed a sigh of relief, walking to where the boatman, Charon, waited with the ferry.

Ambrogio pulled two coins from his pocket and placed them in Charon's skeletal hand. There was no turning back now. As the dead waters of the River Styx flowed by the ferry, Ambrogio swallowed against his fear. He was trapped within the land of the dead, with only his hope that he could make a deal with Hades.

The ferry bumped against the bank and Ambrogio traveled up the path to the Palace of Hades. The empty stares of the ghoulish guards sent shivers down his spine, he summoned his last bit of courage to enter the palace and find his way to the throne room.

"A mortal? A mortal has entered my domain? Why have you come?" Hades asked with curiosity, staring at the man before him. He knew this man had forfeited his life the moment he stepped on the ferry.

"I have fallen in love with the goddess Selene, I ask that you grant me the same immortality she possesses, so that we may be together."

"You fail to mention the curse that Apollo has placed upon you."

"I do not ask any favor in regards to my curse, I only ask that I may live as long as my beloved Selene."

"Be careful what you wish for, mortal."

"Surely you would go to any length for one you love."

Hades looked past Ambrogio and deep into his queen, Persephone's eyes. He sighed, yes, he had also gone to great lengths for his love. "What do you offer?"

"I offer my soul."

CHAPTER SIXTEEN

Satisfaction flowed through Lorelai as the screams of terror echoed in her ears. The awakened members of her coven had flooded into a small local town, overwhelming it, drinking the population dry. The ones who hadn't been feasted upon yet, were locked in houses, waiting to die.

Their screams fell on deaf ears, well not deaf, these pitiful humans didn't realize that predators were drawn to the cries of injured animals, and their cries for help were a lure to every vampire in the area. The more they screamed, the hungrier Lorelai's followers became.

She dropped the body she held in one hand and strode down the street. This was what was meant for her people. They were the superior beings, they were meant to rule this Earth. It did not matter if they must shun the day, the night was their haven, their mother. She looked at the moon and smiled, so much had started with that beautiful, round orb.

The screams turned to whimpers as the vampires finished feeding and prepared to sleep for the day. Tomorrow would be another night, it would soon be time to travel to another town, so they could gather more humans to wake the rest of her sleeping coven. This past week of gluttony and revelry strengthened her first wave, but they couldn't be foolish or allow the outside world to discover them prematurely.

Once they had entered the town, they had disabled any communication with the outside world, a fun little device her minions had created, stopped any type of cell phone or electronic device from working. They had made sure that no one could leave the town, even during the day while they slept, those who attempted escape were the first to be fed upon.

"My Queen, we must rest." Said her minion from behind her.

"Yes, I am just enjoying our perfect little restaurant. What do the humans call it? Farm to fork?" She laughed as she walked into the building to sleep until the next evening. Tomorrow they would send the humans who remained to the nest, while the coven traveled to another town. The Huntress still had not shown herself, perhaps she was finally dead? Today, Lorelai would finally rest easy, secure in her victory and plans for the future.

A short time later, at the edge of the treeline, just outside of town, Mark stood, watching the quiet town. He hadn't been able to reach his grandmother in days, he couldn't even reach her neighbors who checked on her daily. Something was wrong, he looked through his binoculars again. Nothing, no movement, no sounds, no children playing, no dogs barking. By now the town should be busy.

He got down on his belly, crawling toward the nearest building. He felt silly, there had to be a logical explanation, but something about the silence made his skin crawl. He reached the building, he flattened his back against the wall, peering around the corner. His breath caught in his throat, the street was full of bodies, blood ran down the gutter.

He had seen much in his times as an officer but the bile rose in his throat, he swallowed hard against it. He could see his grandmothers house across the street, silent as everything else. He had to know. With every ounce of strength he possessed, he ran across the street to her house, hiding between the bushes and the side wall, while making sure nothing had seen him.

"Mark?" Came a whisper from a window.

"Grandma? What happened here?"

"You must go, get out of here and never come back. They will kill you."

"We have to get you out!"

"No! You must go now. It's too late for me, go!"

"What are they?"

"Vampires." She whimpered as she crumpled to the floor. "Go! Promise me you will go!"

"I..."

"Promise me!"

"I promise." He whispered.

"Never forget, I love you."

Mark cursed as he ran from the town to his car. He had to get back to the station, this needed to be investigated. The air burned his lungs as he ran, his muscles burning, threatening to give out. Rocks flew as he jumped into his car and sped away.

The sun blazed down on the corpses left in the street, filling the air with a putrid smell. The people left gagged as their friends and neighbors began to rot in the street. No breeze lifted the air to give them relief.

As the moon began to rise, Lorelai stepped from the house, well rested and prepared for her next step. As she stepped into the street, she paused and sniffed the air.

"Someone has been visiting. Someone doesn't belong." She turned to her hunter. "Nikolai, where did our visitor go?"

Nikolai followed the fresh scent of unfamiliar human. Soon it led him to the window and the cowering woman inside.

"You have had a visitor old woman?"

"No, no please."

"Nikolai, find him." Lorelai ordered as Nikolai sped off after the scent. Lorelai picked up Mark's grandmother, a cruel smile on her face.

"Please don't kill him."

"Oh, I won't kill him." She laughed. "You will." The grandmother gasped as Lorelai leaned in and bit her neck, then bit her hand and squeezed some of her own dark blood into the woman's mouth.

CHAPTER SEVENTEEN

"What?" Marie said grouchily over her coffee.

"I beg your pardon?" Dr. Ashref replied, his eyebrows raised in surprise.

"You've been studying me ever since we met. Why?" Marie was blunt, she had to know if the man she traveled with could be trusted, or if she would have to find a way to remove him from this equation. She hadn't thought much about his lack of reaction to the existence of vampires, he studied myth after all, but something was off.

Dr. Ashref cleared his throat and laughed uncomfortably. "I thought I was so clever." He pulled an old photo from his jacket pocket. "You look very similar to someone my grandmother used to know. I thought perhaps there was a connection."

Marie picked up the photo and paled slightly, smiling back at her was... well her. "I can see the resemblance." She said, attempting to sound confused. "Don't they say you have six doppelgangers in the world? It seems mine has traveled in time."

"Yes, of course. Silly of me to think otherwise." Dr. Ashref placed the photo back in his pocket and dropped the subject, but Marie's mind was racing. Who was this man and how did he have that picture? Nasira had been a good friend many years ago, but like any who got too close to Marie, she had been killed by Lorelai's followers. Yet this man claimed to be her grandson? Had one of her children survived?

Marie's head began to pound, as she continued to puzzle on the issue. She would watch him to see what his next step would be. So far he had been a good source of information, she may yet need his assistance. They quickly paid the check and loaded their few bags into the car. Riding in companionable silence as Dr. Ashref turned north toward their next destination.

"It seems there is a cavern here," Marie said pointing to the map on her Ipad, "that was once thought to be an entrance to the Underworld. Let's begin our search for the next clue there."

"As long as we don't actually have to enter the Underworld." He quipped back.

"Scared?" Marie said mockingly.

"Cautious, as you should be."

Marie's teasing tone sobered and she focused on the task ahead. She could not get attached to this man, no matter how friendly he was. They needed to find the way into the tomb, so she could find the clues to defeat Lorelai once and for all.

She reached behind her seat, grabbed her small backpack and retrieved the two flashlights she had purchased from the gift shop at the hotel. She inserted the batteries and tested them both.

"Just in case."

They drove as close as the road would take them, but they still had a distance to walk. They shouldered their small packs, then began their trek. As night fell, the cavern loomed in the distance.

"Do you dare to sleep at the entrance to Hell or shall we investigate further?" Marie teased ominously.

Dr. Ashref straightened his shoulders and aimed his beam toward the opening, walking toward it without a backwards glance. Inside the cavern, there was a large dry shelf, alongside the slowly running stream.

"Perhaps we can build a fire and have our supper, while we plan our next steps." Dr. Ashref suggested, removing his pack, rummaging for his sandwich and matches.

The fire burned cheerily, illuminating the cavern while Marie chewed thoughtfully on her sandwich. She scanned the walls of the cavern. Nothing appeared to be altered. The dark cavity at the far side of the cavern beckoned her.

No clue would be hidden at the mouth of the cavern.

The note had said they must follow in Ambrogio's footsteps. That meant they must follow him into the Underworld. Marie stood and began to follow the stream. She heard Dr. Ashref mutter under his breath, but he followed her. His flashlight illuminating her from behind. They scrambled along the narrow passage until it opened into a cavern, a river coursing through it.

"The River Styx?" Dr. Ashref breathed, fear evident in his voice. His eyes darted along the river as if searching for the boatman.

"The gods are dead," Marie said sadly, "as are their ilk." She began to search along the riverbank, her light soon reflecting on an item hidden among the rocks. It was a small, oddly colored box, silver upon closer inspection, that had tarnished in the damp cavern.

"Your seal." Dr. Ashref pointed to the seal on the front of the box. Marie placed her baton against the seal and again its hidden key opened the lock. The lid popped open, inside was an oddly shaped piece of silver. Marie turned it over in her hands, it had indents on the side as if something fit in to it.

"It's a piece of a key, look!" She said pointing at the edges. "Other pieces will fit together to create the key."

"But how many pieces are there?"

"We have no way to know." Marie turned toward the tunnel, ready for the next step of her journey.

CHAPTER EIGHTEEN

1410 BC

"Your soul?" Hades smirked. "Do you not realize that your soul was mine the moment you paid your coins."

Ambrogio looked down at his feet, a sinking feeling in the pit of his stomach. He was losing his chance, he would never see Selene again. What had he done?

"I will do anything you ask, my Lord, but even once I am granted immortality, my soul will be yours for all time."

Hades stood in front of him, his dark eyes boring into Ambrogio, the weight of that stare crushing him. Finally, Hades turned and walked away, sitting on his throne, arching his fingers before him.

"There is a small item I do desire." The god said in a bored tone. "I desire a bow."

"A bow, my Lord?" Hope welled in Ambrogio's chest, a bow was simple, he could make Hades the most beautiful of bows. Ambrogio bowed low. "My Lord Hades, I will craft you the finest bow, of only the best wood. With it you will be the greatest hunter ever."

"Oh, you misunderstand, I do not desire you to make me a bow. I desire a very specific bow. A silver bow."

"The silver bow of Artemis?" Ambrogio whispered, Hades nodded in response.

"What say you, Ambrogio? Do you still wish for your immortality? Or shall you continue on to your fate?" Hades waved his hand and two portals opened. One led back to the mortal world, the temple of Artemis in the distance. The other led to the Elysian Fields, he could see the members of his family, who had long passed waiting for him.

Ambrogio didn't pause to think, but stepped through the portal, emerging at the edge of the woods near the temple. In his mind, he could hear Hades voice. "You have made your choice, your soul is mine for all eternity, you will wander soulless if you fail but you shall never see the Elysian Fields again."

Ambrogio let out a heavy breath and began his trek to the temple. When he arrived at the temple, he kneeled before the altar. "Oh Great Artemis, I come to you a humble man. I have no offering, but I offer myself. I wish to be one of your hunters and serve you all the days of my life."

"A man?" Came a soft voice. "I have never had a man among my hunters before, but your heart seems true. Vow that you shall never touch my maidens and you shall join my hunters."

"I swear with all my soul." Ambrogio kept his eyes down, lest they betray his deceit. He could see the silver bow, held in the hands of the Goddess of the Hunt, Artemis. As he raised his eyes to her, she had a pleasant smile on her face, but he could see cold and cunning behind her eyes.

A wooden bow and quiver of arrows appeared before him. "Take this bow and bring me an offering to prove your loyalty. Though do be quick, sunrise draws nigh and I know of the curse my dear brother placed upon you."

Ambrogio picked up the bow and arrows and bowed low to the goddess, before turning and running out the door toward the forest. Artemis watched with a stony face as the man ran to do her bidding. She would see if he could be trusted.

As the setting moon sparkled on the lake near the temple, Ambrogio saw a pair of swans floating on the water. He quietly took aim and loosed the arrow, striking the swan through the heart. He carefully gathered the bird in his arms, pulling two feathers from its wings before returning to the temple and placing his offering on the altar.

Pleased with his offering, Artemis offered him a safe place

to sleep during the day. Night after night, Ambrogio rose and followed the instructions given to him by Artemis, always leaving her tribute before dawn. Each night he wrote a letter, using the swan feather, to Selene, carefully hiding them away during the day.

One night, as he was writing his letter, he was visited by Persephone. "You ache for the one you love." She said bluntly, Ambrogio nodded. "She aches for you as well." She walked to a nearby tree and placed her hand on it, a small opening appeared. "If you place your letter in this tree, it will appear in one of the trees in the courtyard in Delphi. There your love will find your messages."

Ambrogio hurried to place his letter in the tree, he watched in wonder as it disappeared. "Why do you help me, my lady?"

"I know something about being separated from those I love." She replied as she disappeared into the forest. Ambrogio hurried to find a tribute before the sun rose, but every shot he took missed. Finally, as he watched his last arrow fly past his prey, he fell to his knees, tears of frustration falling.

"Why do you weep, brave hunter?"

"I cannot bring you a tribute, I have failed you tonight."

"You have honored me greatly and gained my trust. You may borrow my bow to hunt your tribute." She handed Ambrogio the bow, the silver gleaming in the moonlight. Ambrogio's breath caught as he took the bow in his hands.

"Thank you, my lady." He had done it! He had the Bow of Artemis. Ambrogio turned and ran into the night.

CHAPTER NINETEEN

Marie watched Dr. Ashref out of the corner of her eye as he turned the key fragment over in his hand, examining every aspect of it. She sped down the road toward their next destination, the Temple of Artemis, but her mind wasn't on the road, it was on the man sitting next to her. She could hear him muttering to himself about the object.

"Silver, yes silver makes sense." He said, so low she almost missed it.

"Why silver?" She questioned him, already knowing the answer, but needing to know how much he knew.

"Hmm?" Dr. Ashref looked up, confused. "Silver? Yes, vampires cannot touch silver you see, it burns their flesh. There have been many tales as to why this occurs, our tale of Ambrogio has a completely new twist on this, but if it is true, then the best and only metal to craft the key pieces out of would be silver."

"Interesting." Marie nodded, curiosity getting the better of her. "Do you know much of vampires then? You knew of them through your studies, but do you actually believe them to be real?"

Dr. Ashref took a deep breath and let it out slowly. "It has long been an interest of my family to study myths and their origins. Through the study of myth, we can see that all myths are based in some form of reality, some more than others. I suppose, though, the more important question is, do you believe?"

"I don't know what I believe anymore." Marie muttered and Dr. Ashref knew this comment extended far past the current topic.

"Then perhaps this trip will help you restore your faith."

Marie nodded, her throat tight, in this short amount of time, she had become closer to this man than she had with any human in centuries. He felt like a father figure to her and that was dangerous, for both of them. She was becoming more human, a hazard in her line of work. She knew, for his safety, she would need for them to go their separate ways, but how? He knew where she was going and he was invested in the mystery now. She would just have to take extra care until they returned to Alexandria and found the temple. Then they would part ways, hopefully he would remain safe.

The miles sped by and soon they came to the ruins of the Temple of Athena, it was well after dark so they booked two adjoining rooms at a local hotel and enjoyed a quiet dinner.

The next morning, they traveled to the ruins, there truly wasn't much to see, a pillar, some crumbled stone, most of it lost to time and weather.

"Where do we start?" Dr. Ashref asked, clearly at a loss. Marie paced the grounds, thinking of the letter and the story.

"In the story, Artemis granted Ambrogio a safe place to sleep during the day... It stands to reason that would be underground. Perhaps we can still find that room?"

"It's as good a plan as any." Dr. Ashref began looking at the ground. "Perhaps if we pace the ground in sections as if we were surveying? We can overlap each other and hopefully not miss anything in this mess."

Together they walked to the edge of the site and began walking slowly back and forth across the ground, looking at every dip and crevice. As the sun sunk low, nothing had caught their eye, they decided to admit defeat for the day and return to the hotel. While Dr. Ashref enjoyed a hot shower, Marie called Roger to check in. He had not made much headway on the location of the temple, but he had secured diving equipment and the proper permits for exploration and excavation, if needed.

Marie hung up the phone, her heart was heavy, she knew how important this quest was, but every new portion of the trip seemed harder than the last. What if the room had been destroyed? What if they couldn't find all the pieces of the key or what if they did and couldn't find the temple? Marie pushed the thoughts from her mind as she laid down to rest.

The next day found them searching the ruins again, as noon came, Marie sat down heavily on a stone, frustrated. Dr. Ashref walked over to join her, his foot catching on a root and tripping him. He caught himself with the stick he had picked up as a cane, but as the large stick struck the stone slab in front of her, it made an oddly hollow sound. Marie raised an eyebrow and knelt down, examining the slab more closely. She pulled a small brush from her back pocket, brushing away the debris, revealing the seal they had been waiting for and they released a collective breath.

Using the baton, she released the lock, grinding could be heard beneath the stone and then it lifted a few inches above the ground, just enough for them to push it away to reveal the stairway below. The air was stale, but not unbreathable, they descended the stairs into the small room below. It wasn't much, four walls and a small cot.

Marie looked around the room. "He was here once upon a time."

"So it would seem."

Marie glanced under the cot, there in the corner was another silver box. She pulled it out, opening the lid, revealing the next key portion and handed it to Dr. Ashref. "Well Dalil, two down, who knows how many to go. Are you ready for the next step in this adventure? Or are you ready to go home?"

"Home? You couldn't send me home if vampires themselves were here. We are in this together." He replied with a fiery challenge in his eyes.

"That's what I thought you'd say." Said Marie as she walked to the stairs. "On to Athens."

CHAPTER TWENTY

1410 BC

Ambrogio ran, on and on, searching frantically for the entrance to the Underworld. Electricity crackled through the air, in a flash of light, Artemis appeared before him, knocking him to the ground. "Why do you run so far, faithful hunter?" She asked, anger filling her voice. "Do you betray me?"

Ambrogio trembled before her. "Forgive me. I had no choice. I offered my soul to Hades in exchange for immortality to be with my love. He asked for your bow."

"Then you have made a poor arrangement." She said, eyes flashing. "You shall be punished for your insolence."

Ambrogio cried out as the silver bow burned his hands, the pain causing it to fall to the ground. Artemis retrieved her bow, then turned to walk away. "Please, please forgive me. I was a fool to betray you." Ambrogio said, tears of defeat and humiliation streaming down his face, the smell of his burnt flesh hanging in the air.

"You betrayed my brother Apollo for this woman, you betray me for this woman. In order to earn your forgiveness, you must forsake this woman." Artemis cried out. "You will forget her, you will make yourself pure of body and mind as the rest of my hunters are, you are never to wed or touch a female. Selene will be lost to you forever. If you show yourself true to me, then you will gain your absolution."

Ambrogio's heart broke, he had failed. He had made deals with the gods and he had lost. Ambrogio wept bitter tears, then raised his hands to the sky. "I pledge my body and mind to only you great Goddess Artemis. I will prove worthy of you."

"Then retire to your chamber. Tomorrow, we begin anew." Artemis disappeared, Ambrogio slowly returned to the temple in defeat. His sleep was plagued with dreams of Hades, 'Your soul belongs to me', he whispered.

"No!" Screamed Ambrogio, startling from his slumber. "I will succeed Hades." He whispered to the darkness.

Time passed slowly, but as the days and months crept by, Ambrogio proved himself to be a great hunter, Artemis slowly gave him her trust. Over time, she began to bestow gifts upon him as her favorite. She gave him heightened senses, strength and speed. Next, she gave him fangs and claws, to fight like the animals, and increased healing. Finally, she gave him the power to change form as she did. While her power was to change into a deer, he belonged to the night, so she granted him the ability to change into a bat.

"You have done well, Ambrogio." Artemis said to him one night. "You have proven yourself in every way, your skills surpass all but my own. But even now I feel the tug of your love for Selene." Ambrogio tried to deny it but Artemis held up her hand. "Do not deny it, but I will grant you one final gift." She held up a leather wrapped package and looked at him sadly. "Take this to Hades and claim your love."

Ambrogio grasped the package containing the silver bow humbled. He bowed low to Artemis. "Thank you kindest of all Goddesses." He backed away slowly and returned to the Underworld.

As he walked into the throne room of Hades with his prize, Hades looked at his changed form. "I grant you immortality to be with your love, but remember Ambrogio, be careful what you wish for." Hades took the bow and held his hand out toward Ambrogio, the man's body began to glow, then the glow faded, Ambrogio felt different. "Your soul is now mine for eternity."

A portal opened to the Temple of Apollo, Ambrogio walked through, emerging into the soft moonlight. He could not wait to find Selene, to tell her they could be together forever. Years had passed but he knew their love was true. Ambrogio approached the temple, his step light, his heart happy.

From inside he heard soft weeping, he saw the girl, now grown into a woman, who had helped him the day he had come for his prophecy. "Why do you weep, my lady?" He asked softly.

Ohanna gasped at the strange appearance of the man before her. "My friend." She said brokenly. "She fell in love with a strange man from far away, he left her broken hearted, but she betrayed her vows to Apollo, she was punished and cursed. She lost her immortality, now she lays dying."

"Selene." Whispered Ambrogio.

CHAPTER TWENTY ONE

1407 BC

Ambrogio crept into the temple, unseen. He could hear her heartbeat, slow and faltering. As he entered her room, he saw her lying on her cot, her eyes closed, her breathing shallow and ragged. He took her into his arms, kissing her temple, she was far past any recognition.

"We will be together, my love." He whispered as he stole her away into the darkness. Ambrogio used every gift he had been given by the goddess Artemis to bring his love to her temple before Selene's time expired. "Artemis!" He cried out. "Save her." He placed her motionless body on the altar.

"I cannot save her." Artemis said softly.

"But you are a goddess, you can do anything."

Artemis laughed. "In many cases that is true, but she is cursed by my brother. I cannot defy his will."

"Cannot or will not? You knew when you gave me the bow."

"Yes, I did, now I will offer you the chance to save her. As your final act of loyalty to me. You must bite her, drink her blood, then have her drink yours. She will become as you are. By doing this, you shall save her life, though I warn you, her mortal body will be dead, her soul shall belong to the moon, she will live again as the Goddess of the Moon."

"And we will be immortal together." He said as he leaned in.

"You will both be immortal, but you will not be together. Your vows to me must be upheld, she will belong to the Moon, should she choose to leave, she will lose her soul and embrace only darkness."

"Selene will never be dark, she is only the light. I vow to follow your teachings all the rest of my life, only allow me to save her." Ambrogio could hear Selene's heartbeat growing fainter. Artemis stepped back as he leaned in again, his fangs puncturing her neck, her warm blood cascading down his throat.

So sweet, he drank as a dying man in the desert, the blood calmed a thirst he had never known existed. He needed more, but all too soon it was gone. He bit his own lip, thick blood oozing from the wound. He leaned in to kiss her, the only kiss they would ever share, forcing the thick blood past her lips. As he watched, she changed becoming more like he was. Her eyes fluttered open, she stared into his eyes.

"Ambrogio?" She questioned reaching for him, but Artemis stepped in, with a wave of her hands, Selene began to glow. Her glowing form floated out the window, into the night, toward the moon.

"You have saved your love, she is safe from any further interference from my brother so long as she stays where I have bid her."

Ambrogio's head swarmed with need, the blood was not enough. He thirsted for more, his throat burned with a need that only blood could quench. He bowed low to Artemis, quickly he left her temple, it was time to hunt, only this time he hunted something new. He hunted humans.

Ambrogio looked up at the soft glow of the moon and saw the face of his love. "I will create more in your image my love, I will create children for you to love." Ambrogio disappeared into the shadows, that night the blood did run as the Oracle had foreseen.

CHAPTER TWENTY TWO

The visit and escape of the unknown human unsettled Lorelai. Had the Huntress found a human ally? How did he elude her greatest tracker? She would have to regroup. It was not yet time for the world to know of their existence, she had celebrated too soon, it had come back to bite her, and she was the one who was supposed to do the biting.

"Burn the town, leave no trace of our existence. Make it look like an accident." Lorelai commanded, looking at the power station at the edge of town. She could hear gasps and cries from the humans held hostage in the buildings. "We return to the nest, and don't forget to bring a snack." Her lips curled in a cruel smile as the humans were led from the buildings and tied together in a line to be led back to the nest. True, she could have enthralled them, but that would be nice, she didn't feel like playing nice, she wanted someone to suffer.

She ran her sharp nail down the arm of the man nearest her, drawing blood that she licked away, smirking at the smell of fear that oozed from him. "Don't worry little lamb," she purred mockingly, "it will all be over soon, you will be the perfect snack for one of my coven."

The man sneered at her, spitting in her face. Lorelai slapped him, knocking him off his feet, her followers closed in, ready to feed on the wounded man. Lorelai held up her hand, she had found her focus. "No, he will be spared, but he will not find respite as the others will when we reach the nest. He will be hung on the hook, for all to use, he will not be drained, he will continue to suffer for as long as I see fit."

Lorelai grabbed him by the arm, picking him off the ground, breaking his arm in the process. She heard his sharp intake of breath, but no other sound was uttered. Good, he would be a challenge, while some enjoyed a good book, Lorelai enjoyed cracking a persons deepest fears, finding every way to destroy a human, before she finally let them die a painful death. It had been so long since she had allowed herself a plaything, but this man had decided his own fate.

Behind them, a series of loud explosions could be heard, slightly shaking the ground. Her minions had ignited the power station, creating the illusion that the ensuing fire and destruction had ruptured and ignited the gas lines that ran under the town. By morning, the entire town would be burned to ash. They were far enough from another town that an alarm wouldn't be raised, and no one was left here to tell the tale.

Lorelai looked into the sky, the weather had been unseasonably warm, but finally the clouds were pooling in the sky, it looked like there would be a snow storm tonight. It was closing in on the end of November, it was soon to be what these Americans called 'Thanksgiving', Lorelai knew what she had to be thankful for this year, as long as she could keep her secret from getting out too early.

Lorelai looked at the string of humans trudging along the path her followers had set. Perhaps she should hold on to them, her coven should have a Thanksgiving dinner after all. She would need to find more for it to be a proper feast, her smile turned cunning. With this change in the weather, she wouldn't have to work hard at all.

She beckoned to her grumpy minion, he already knew her plan. He gathered his brothers and disappeared into the darkness. The main city was full of people the humans called homeless, they would be looking for food and a warm bed during the storm, and Lorelai was always willing to care for a lost lamb. Her minions would play the part of the valiant social workers, give out the directions to the nest, which was always disguised as an unassuming ranch, they might even 'borrow' a bus to bring them in. Lorelai laughed at how gullible people could be when they thought something was free. Well, she would feed her new flock and prepare them for the true feast... Them.

The moon reflected in Lorelai's eyes as her plan took place in her mind. They might not be able to continue as planned, but she would be able to awaken her coven just as easily this way, even more so do to the fortuitous storm. The wind blew past Lorelai, caressing her cheek, a crack of thunder boomed in the distance as if agreeing with her. Her mouth watered as she envisioned her coming Thanksgiving surprise.

CHAPTER TWENTY THREE

1407 BC

Ohanna shuttered the windows against the night, a new practice in the temple. Recently there had been people going missing or even bodies found. She shuddered as she looked at Selene's empty cot, at the memory of the strange man she had seen just prior to her disappearance. Had Selene been one of the victims? Was that man behind her disappearance, perhaps all of these new attacks?

Ohanna sighed and began to collect Selene's effects from the small chamber. The Oracle had changed since her sisters' curse and later disappearance. She rarely spoke, her prophecies had gotten sparse, she denied that her sister was gone. This morning, she had finally come to terms with her grief, she had asked Ohanna to dispose of her sisters' items, then prepare the room for herself, to take over as the Oracle's helper.

Ohanna had placed everything into a basket to send to the orphanage, then grabbed the mattress to take it outside to hang in the fresh air. She felt an odd shape inside as she picked it up. There was a small hole in the edge of the mattress, she carefully reached in, her hand connecting with parchment. Ohanna pulled the sheets out, her eyes going wide as she read them. 'I promise I will find a way to be together', 'I have made a deal with Hades' the author had written. Every detail of the terrifying change documented.

Ohanna's hand flew to her mouth as she read the

signature scrawled across the bottom of the parchment. "Ambrogio!" Ohanna remembered the strange man who had stolen Selene's heart, she saw the empty look in Selene's eyes when he had disappeared, she remembered the anger of Apollo and how he had cursed Selene. Then Ohanna remembered the strange man from the night of Selene's disappearance, she knew that it was Ambrogio, changed to a terrifying form.

She remembered his fangs and the marks on the body she had seen in town. He had become the monster that preyed on the town. She looked at the pages again, she had the secret to stopping him. She had to tell the guards. Ohanna raced from the temple, the precious parchment pages gripped in her hands. She ran until she found two guards, they always traveled in groups now as a precaution against the beast.

"I know how to stop the creature." She panted, out of breath from her run, thrusting the pages toward the older guard. "Sunlight, silver. We can stop him."

"What are you going on about, girl? Get back in the temple. It isn't safe to be out alone after dark!" The older guard gently pushed her toward the temple. The younger guard looked at her in sympathy.

"No, you don't understand! Your weapons can't hurt it."

"Take her back to the temple. Make sure she gets rest, it seems she is overwrought." Ohanna struggled as the younger guard guided her back to the temple. "And make sure she does not leave the temple again tonight." The older guard called after them.

Ohanna could hear soft laughter in her head as she walked in the moonlight. "You will never stop him." She heard Selene's voice whisper to her. "I will be watching you." Ohanna looked around, she saw nothing, the only person was the young guard walking next to her.

"Did you hear something?"

The guard looked confused, perhaps the temple maiden was unwell. He knew nothing of the temple, but he had heard tales of the prophecies and the Oracle. Perhaps this maiden was more than she seemed. He shook his head in response, he held the temple door open, then positioned himself outside to guard the temple for the night.

The next morning an alarm was sounded from the town. The older guard had been found in the street, his throat ripped out, the latest victim of the beast. Ohanna knew no one would believe her. She took a deep breath and walked to the altar. Placing the parchment on the altar, she kneeled before it.

"Oh Great Apollo, I renounce my vows to you. I leave this temple, to fight the evil that was created by your curse. I do not ask your permission, nor beg your forgiveness, I only ask that you let me be, to complete my task."

The sky rumbled and a single ray of sunlight fell on her shoulders. Ohanna felt at peace, she retrieved the pieces of parchment, then left the temple. Never to return.

CHAPTER TWENTY FOUR

1407 BC

Ohanna had taken everything of hers from the temple, leaving no trace that she had ever existed, she traveled to the one place she hoped could help. She only traveled by daylight, the memory of Selene's voice in her head a chilling thought. Every night she read the letters again, every word cementing her resolve. Tales of horrors followed her travels as Ambrogio and his followers grew in numbers.

At last the city of Athens stood tall on the horizon. The great Temple of Athena proudly overlooking all. Ohanna swallowed against the fear welling up inside her. What if the goddess would not hear her plea? She would be truly alone to face this darkness.

As the sun reached its zenith, Ohanna climbed the steps and bowed before the altar. She pulled from her bag a small carved owl, a gift from her father, now her only offering to the goddess. She placed the token on the altar and prayed.

"Great Goddess Athena, I come before you to ask your aide. Not for myself, but for all of humanity. A terrible monster has been created, it has taken my friend, killed many of my town, and seeks to create more like itself. I have the knowledge to destroy the creature, but not the skill. I ask that you make me a warrior, so that I may fight this demon, to protect the people."

Ohanna crumpled to the ground, spent. Her eyes glued to the base of the altar. Athena was her only hope, she had the wisdom to see the truth in her words and the ability to train her as a warrior to defeat Ambrogio and his minions. Her body ached, yet still she remained kneeling at the altar, waiting for a response. The sun hung low in the sky and still she waited, her body crying out in pain.

The butt of Athena's spear struck the stones in front of Ohanna, but she did not flinch, she held true to her belief and her plea. She raised her face to the goddess, looking her in the eyes.

"Help me save them." She pleaded. Athena held out her hand.

"Show me the letters." Ohanna retrieved the letters from her bag and handed them to the goddess. "What has been created cannot be defeated by you alone."

"I will help her." The young guard stepped from the shadows, all this time he had followed her, fulfilling his last order to keep her safe. "That demon killed my father. He should have believed you when you said you knew the way to defeat them and it cost him his life. I will avenge him."

Athena nodded as the guard stepped forward. "Your name, soldier."

"Alek." He bowed to the women.

"Ohanna and Alek, Ambrogio has created others. I will not make the same mistake as Apollo and Artemis, I will not grant you gifts of the gods. But I will train you, and your first lesson begins now." She pointed to the road approaching the temple. Two vampires ran toward the temple, blood dripping from their mouths, their eyes wild.

Athena handed Ohanna a silver sword, to Alek she gave her own silver spear. "Through the heart only, then you must remove the head."

Ohanna stepped forward nervously, the only blade she had held was the dinner knife at meals, she had never killed any creature. Alek moved alongside her, holding the spear confidently in his hand.

"I believe in you." He said before moving forward, thrusting the spear at the first vampire. It dodged his attack but he swung around and caught it in the back, it hissed as the spear punctured its chest. Its partner growled as it lunged toward Ohanna, a small scream escaped her as she swung the sword, she could feel the breeze from its claws as they just missed her face.

A soft laugh echoed on the breeze. "You'll never win." Selene whispered.

Ohanna steeled herself as she turned toward the creature, blood still dripped from its fangs as it advanced on her. Ohanna focused on its chest, on the spot where its heart would be, she raised the sword and plunged forward. Her breath caught as she felt the weapon connect and sink into the flesh.

On the hill behind them, a figure turned and fled into the night. A scream filled the air, Selene howled in rage. "You killed my children. You will never be safe, I will not rest until you are destroyed."

"You are nothing now, only a whisper on the breeze. But I will not rest until every one of your children are destroyed. No matter how long it takes," she looked at Alek and he nodded his agreement, "we will make sure that our children know your secrets, and they teach it to their children. If it takes until the end of time, you will be defeated."

CHAPTER TWENTY FIVE

Marie leafed through the pages of the tale of Ambrogio again, in the back of her mind she doubted her decision to travel there. The account of his travels never specifically said he traveled there, it was so vague, but it did say that Ohanna had learned how to fight the demons from Athena herself, so the next logical destination in their journey would be the Temple of Athena. If they were wrong, they would have to retrace their steps, Marie prayed she was correct.

"We have to examine every lead." Dalil said as if reading her mind. "I have read that script as many times as you have, it mentions Athens and Athena, even if it isn't in conjunction with Ambrogio, it has to be a clue or why would they have included it?"

Marie could see a cloud of doubt in his furrowed brow. "It also says 'follow the path of Ambrogio', not Ohanna. What if this is just to throw us off the trail?"

"Why would your ancestors do that? Wouldn't they want you to succeed?"

"Maybe it's a test of how well we follow instructions." Marie ran a hand down her face, frustration rising as each mile passed. She turned her face to the window, a small rain storm had started at some point, she watched the raindrops etch their way across the window. Never before had she doubted herself so much, before she always felt like she had time, but now she felt like it was just slipping away.

The steady sound of the storm lulled her to sleep and she

drifted off in the uncomfortable car seat. Dark dreams plagued her, memories of her grandmother, her husband, and always the mocking eyes of Lorelai. She jerked awake, something in her dream startling her, she looked around. The passing road sign indicated it was only a few more kilometers to Athens.

"You should have woken me, it was my turn to drive."

"You needed the rest more." Country gave way to the busy streets of Athens, the sun peeked through the clouds, a single beam resting on the temple. "Perhaps the gods send us a good omen then." Chuckled Dalil.

"We will take all the good luck we can get." Marie replied with a nod. The doubt was still firmly settled in her stomach, but Dalil's good humor was quickly banishing it. Ironic, how just yesterday he was solely 'Dr. Ashref' in her mind and yet today, he had slipped into the familiarity of a first name basis.

Marie looked at the large structure, the only one so far that was more than crumbled ruins. She wondered if it was truly all original or if some skilled craftsmen had reconstructed it over the centuries. She had never visited this area enough to notice any changes. Visitors traveled amongst the columns and into the large inner chamber.

Dalil parked the car, then walked around to open her door, offering his elbow as he did. "Shall we, my dear? With so many tourists, we don't want to draw attention to ourselves. Today, we should be as they are, simply here to observe."

Marie slipped her hand into the crook of his elbow, for all intents and purposes, they gave the illusion of a father and daughter exploring the temple. Marie's sharp eyes wandered the columns and walls of the temple... nothing.

"It's too obvious here, we need to find a place more hidden."

"Or more obvious..." Dalil gently guided her out of the temple, positioning her so she faced the temple, while appearing to be in idle conversation. "Look at the temple, at the raised dais at the left side."

"Athena! Do you truly think they would hide it in such an

obvious place?"

"The dais is closed to visitors..."

"But not to us." Marie retorted with a wicked gleam in her eye. They slowly walked around the outside of the temple, watching for guards or other visitors. When they we sure they weren't watching they climbed to the top of the dais, making sure to stay on their bellies, so to not attract attention.

"While I don't want to get caught, I'm glad we didn't have to do that climb in the dark." Dalil said, wiping his skinned palms on his trousers.

Marie crawled forward, looking at each of the statues of Athena. Wrong, she was wrong, there was nothing here. Marie rested her head on the cool rock, exhausted. Back to the drawing board, they would have to decipher the story again.

"We will find the next clue, it's a big temple, we can't have searched everything yet." Dalil assured her as he turned to crawl back to the edge. The clouds had been playing peekaboo with the sun and a small shaft of light struck the base of one of the statues as he turned, drawing his attention. "She knelt at her feet." He whispered, crawling forward to look again.

There at the base of the statue, nestled between Athena's feet was the crest. The lock for another clue. Marie inserted the baton and turned. A narrow section of stone dropped down, almost taking Dalil with it, revealing a shallow coffer containing a small silver box and a gleaming silver spear. Marie drew a sharp breath.

"Could it be? The Spear of Athena?"

CHAPTER TWENTY SIX

Marie looked at the spear, shining in the soft sunlight. Could it truly be the Spear of Athena? She reached out a shaking hand to touch the cool metal. It was beautiful, perfectly crafted, perfectly balanced, a true weapon of destruction.

Dalil looked at the sun, still hanging lazily in the sky, peeking in and out of the clouds as they blew across the heavens. He reached into his pocket, pulling out a couple bags of trail mix and pretzels that he had saved from the plane.

"There's no way we will get that to the car with all of these witnesses. Our only chance is to wait until darkness, then try to get down safely." He tore open a bag of pretzels and began to munch quietly. Marie ignored the food and her protesting stomach, reaching into the opened space, retrieving the silver box. She knew it contained the next piece of the key, she hoped it was the final piece, as they had no more clues to follow.

The lid creaked open, inside, wrapped in a parchment was the next piece of the key. Marie sighed heavily, she could tell by looking at the shape of the piece, that it was not the final one. There were more, but where? The parchment fluttered in the soft breeze, Marie noticed faded writing.

'You have done well, my descendant.
I know nothing of you, but you have
followed the clues we have given
you well. The next portion of your
journey begins now and will become
even more dangerous. As you reach
the answers to how to defeat the

children of Ambrogio and Selene,
she will awaken and take notice.
You will not be safe until she is
destroyed.'

Marie paused in her reading and groaned. Great, another vampire queen to kill. Would this one be more powerful than Lorelai? How would they destroy both? Dalil nudged her shoulder and urged her to open the parchment so they could continue.

'After Ohanna and Alek destroyed
the vampires that had followed
them, Ambrogio fled to his home.
He came from a small village on the
Peninsula Italia, he slowly created
more like himself, always calling
them his children. He founded
the first coven of vampires. This
coven took refuge in an ancient
lagoon, too swampy for humans,
but perfect for the vampires.
There, they built a city, which
they called Tutum. Vampires
still inhabit this city as I write
this letter, but that is your next
destination, take this spear for
safety. I fear to send you on
this errand, but there are
answers that lie only in this
location. Be safe and bring an
end to this all.'

A shiver ran down Marie's spine as she finished the letter and looked at Dalil. "Tutum? I have not heard of this city." He said as he adjusted himself to a more comfortable position.

"I have." Marie sighed. "It was known as Tutum to only

the vampires, but as the years passed and the city grew, more humans came to live there. It exists today, but it is known as Venice."

"Ah, there are many ties to Venice in the vampire legends."

"For good reason it would seem."

The sun dipped below the horizon and the last of the tourists filed out of the site, leaving Marie and Dalil cold and exposed on top of the dais.

"Climb down first, I will hand it to you." Dalil offered, worry showing on his face at the thought of the perilous climb down the side of the crumbling dais. Marie nodded, she wished they had thought to bring a flashlight, but all she had was the light on her phone. The moon was little help, Marie was thankful for her enhanced vision as she slowly traversed the crumbling rock.

"Ok, I'm down." She called softly, stretching up for the spear. It barely brushed her fingertips as he held it over the edge for her. "Drop it. I can catch it."

Doubt shadowed Dalil's face as he let the spear slip from his hand and fall the few feet to Marie. He let out his breath in a soft whoosh of air as she gracefully caught it, then shone the small light of the phone on an area for him to use as a foothold. Painstakingly slow was his descent, but every step of the way, Marie guided him until he reached the bottom.

"On to Venice then?" He said, his voice slightly breathless with the effort. They turned toward the car as a bright light shone in their faces.

"Where do you think you're going?"

CHAPTER TWENTY SEVEN

"I said, where do you think you're going?" The guard looked at the large spear in Marie's hand. "Stealing from an archaeological site are we? Hands against the wall, you're under arrest."

"My good sir," Dalil began, "this can all be easily explained. If you would just..."

"I said, against the wall." The guard ordered as he shoved Dalil against the wall, causing the older man to stumble and fall.

"Leave him alone." Marie growled, low and deadly.

"Or what?"

Marie looked at Dalil struggling to regain his footing. Or what? She couldn't do anything too exciting and reveal anything to Dalil. She placed the spear on the ground by her feet, then quickly swung her leg around, connecting with his temple with a satisfying thud. Slowly the guard crumpled to the ground, Marie held out her hand to Dalil.

"Go get the car, we need to leave quickly. I'll make sure he's safe." Dalil looked at Marie, then at the unconscious guard, then back at Marie questioningly. "What? I work out." Marie rolled her eyes, she watched as he walked to the car, then she turned to the guard. She bent over and whispered into his ear. "You fell and hit your head, you will remember nothing of this encounter." She carefully moved him to a safer area of the site, returning to the car, after retrieving the spear. "We should go quickly before he wakes."

"He will come after us when he does."

"Perhaps he will forget."

"One can only hope." Dalil said absently as he sped away. "See if you can get some tickets to Venice. I do not fancy the drive."

Marie quickly booked two tickets to Venice, a red-eye, in coach. She prayed the guard hadn't called in a description of their vehicle, it could easily be traced back to them. While she had an alias that could easily be changed, Dalil did not. She called Roger quickly, requesting that he send the proper paperwork ahead to the airport to transport the spear as an archaeological treasure, they stopped briefly to find packaging for the valuable item. She breathed a sigh of relief as they checked the vehicle in and boarded the plane with no issues. Soon, the lights of the City of Water, Venice, were below them.

They rented a car, driving through the quiet city, toward a small cafe. "Where do we even start?" Dalil mused. "Everything else has been so clear, a set destination. Here we have an entire city to explore."

"This is your area of expertise. What to the legends say about the vampires of Venice?"

"Never anything concrete about a location." Dalil noticed a man standing on the side of the road, an old carriage waiting, with a small sign on the side of it. 'Tours of Venice, see the dark side of the city', Dalil slowed the car and looked at Marie. "What better place to start than with a tour of the city."

Marie glanced at him with a dare in her eye. "You trust an odd man in the middle of the night to give you a tour of the city? While we are looking for vampires?" She laughed. "You are braver than I gave you credit for."

They left the vehicle, taking the package containing the spear and approached the carriage. "Ah, my good man, my daughter fancies a tour of the city." He chuckled. "She wants to see the vampires." He winked conspiratorially at the man, as a father humoring his daughter's whim.

"You want to see vampires? I'll show you vampires." The man's deep voice was dead and chilling, he eyed the long box in

Marie's hands. "There's no room for that."

Marie hugged the box tightly and pouted, playing the part of the indulged child. "It's a present for Mother, I couldn't bear to part with it. Something could happen to it."

The man glanced at the box again. "Suit yourself, but if anything happens, don't say you weren't warned." If Marie was any other girl, she might have been intimidated by this man, but she had dealt with far worse than a con man and a thief in her lifetime. They climbed into the carriage, watching the passing scenery as their guide began his tour.

Nothing exciting, a few cemeteries, an old tunnel, a crumbling church. Nothing that seemed to show any actual sign of where they needed to be. Finally, they pulled in front of an old mansion, far on the edge of town and stopped. The guide turned around, his fangs gleaming in the moonlight.

"Now we come to the end of our tour."

CHAPTER TWENTY EIGHT

"Look out Allison." Dalil yelled as he threw himself in front of Marie, but Marie just sat there, her shoulders shaking with laughter.

"It's okay." She whispered softly as she pushed past him to stand up. Looking at the driver, her eyes cold, she kicked him in the chest, knocking him from his seat to the ground with a painful thud. She was weary of this game of cat and mouse, searching for piece after piece, she needed answers NOW, and no costume shop fanged freak would stand in her way.

She moved like a lynx, deadly and cunning, advancing on the terrified driver, even Dalil eyed her wearily as she pulled the broken baton from beneath her coat. She held the weapon to the drivers neck, as she thought, no burning, this man was no vampire, he only pretended to be one as part of his tour.

"Per favore," he sputtered, lapsing into his native tongue in fear, "please, I meant no harm, only a bit of fear, it makes the tour fun."

"I do not care about your fun. I asked for vampires, and you have failed to deliver more than a dime store charlatan. Can you show me vampires or not?"

Fear flicked across the mans face again. "No." Marie shoved the man away angrily, this had all been a waste of time, she turned back to the carriage, intent on taking it and leaving this man to the darkness. "Please, no one has seen vampires here for many years, but this house was one of their homes." She locked him with a steely glare. "I swear to you, signora, I would not lie."

"But you would pretend to be a vampire?"

"That was no lie, only part of my story, a story you did not allow me to finish."

"Then pray tell me your story and be quick about it." Marie growled as she raised the baton to his neck again. The man nodded his head and began.

"Long ago, before the city was more than swamp land, a man lived in a small village near here. He had great aspirations but no drive so he decided to venture far from home to visit the great Oracle at Delphi. He was gone for many years, no one knew what his fate was, fewer cared, but when he returned he had changed. He found the lowest of the low in society, he made them like him, evil, bloodthirsty. Finally, they built this house deep in the swamp, they created the first coven of vampires. It was a dark and dangerous time, no one knew what vampires were, let alone know how to defeat them, so the coven grew in darkness, and in secret. All of those secrets have been lost, save this house. Over the centuries it was rebuilt and expanded to house his growing coven, blood flowed and people feared for their lives, then one day, poof," he made an exploding gesture with his hands, "they disappeared without a trace. Some say a powerful vampire queen rose and took them somewhere safe so they could take over the world, others say a hunter destroyed them all. We will never truly know, most of the story has been lost to time, even his name."

"Ambrogio." Marie whispered.

"What? Have you heard this tale before?" Marie ignored him and walked toward the locked gate, grabbing her wrapped package as she did. "Wait, you can't go in there, that's trespassing."

Marie arched an eyebrow. "Are you going to stop me?"

"No." He mumbled in response.

"Wait with the carriage."

"You can't leave me here alone."

Dalil chuckled. "I thought you liked a good scare, and you

said there hadn't been real vampires here for years."

The man shuffled his feet and looked at the ground as Marie used her baton to break the lock. The rusty chain fell to the ground, as the ancient gate creaked open slightly. There was enough moon to light their way, but it was still dark and creepy. Their feet sloshed in the water of the driveway, the swamp seeming to attempt to reclaim this part of the land, in stark contrast to the beautiful city not far away.

Marie paused. "All we need now is a blast of lightning to complete the mood." She quipped and the driver shuddered. The wooden stairs were rotten as they tread carefully across the porch to the front door. The wood creaked dangerously under their feet as it threatened to give way.

"At least the house appears more sturdy." Dalil observed, his voice hushed, fear tickling his spine.

The door was slightly ajar and Marie pushed it open, leaves had blown across the floor, showing the years of neglect and disuse.

"Now, where to begin?"

CHAPTER TWENTY NINE

Lorelai looked out the window of the farmhouse, the early twilight of the late November evening still glistening on the snow. Below her, she could hear the milling of her followers waking and preparing for the evening. On this night the humans called 'Thanksgiving', they would indeed give thanks for all they had, and everything they would be claiming soon.

Their guests of honor, or dinner, were quietly waiting in a room below, compelled into submission, Lorelai had no desire for the screaming and crying to disrupt her night of revelry. The pigs would indeed eat well tonight, but there would be too many bodies for them to dispose of them all, so Lorelai had the humans dig their own mass grave. Cruel? Perhaps, but the humans were little better than pigs themselves.

She turned from the window and walked to her closet, glancing through the rack of designer clothing. Tonight was special and she needed to dress for the occasion. She pulled a black dress from the closet, tight, plunging neckline, no sleeves, formal enough for the event but the style ensured ease and cleanliness when she fed tonight. She did hate to get blood on her clothes.

She pulled her dark hair back and secured it with a diamond comb, preening in front of the mirror before turning away satisfied. She descended the stairs, a regal vision, as beautiful as her storybook counterpart, if only her character had been evil at heart. As she entered the main dining room of the nest, she appreciated the festive decorations and the beautifully presented table. Not that they needed the plates and cutlery, but it added that special something to their feast.

Others from her coven milled about the room, resplendent in their finery as well. They bowed to her as she entered the room. In the corner, stoically stood their feast, the charm was still in place, so they knew no fear, but soon, Lorelai would release them and their fear would resonate through the building, causing every vampire to feed with a frenzy.

Lorelai had been sure to personally select only the best of their flock for the dinner. The others, the children and elderly, were held elsewhere for meals when the rest of the coven was awakened. For now, they would rest and enjoy the spoils of their first small victory. By now, she was sure that the devastation of the town had been discovered, but she knew the police would not be led here.

She smiled as she raised a glass of blood-tinged wine to the others in the room.

"A toast to all we have accomplished in this short time and all we shall become in the future. The world is ours and we shall claim it!"

Roars of agreement resounded through the room as the rest of the vampires joined in on the toast. Lorelai gestured for the crowd to take their place at the table, then compelled their meals to come forward. One victim for every vampire, as the humans stood next to the chairs, Lorelai snapped her fingers.

"Freeze and awaken." The humans blinked their eyes, some screamed, others began to cry.

"I can't move."

"What's happening."

"We're all going to die." A woman hysterically sobbed.

"We are thankful for the sacrifice you are willing to make to nourish our bodies, so that we may continue toward our glorious future, and to reclaim what is rightfully ours." Lorelai reached for her human, forcing him onto the table, then leapt onto him with gusto, drinking deeply. The others soon joined in as the remaining humans cowered in the corner, unable to move, waiting to know their fate.

Lorelai daintily wiped the blood from her mouth and looked mockingly at the rest of the humans.

“Seconds anyone?”

CHAPTER THIRTY

Marie stepped into the darkness, the mustiness of the air overwhelming. As a vampires house, it could have been much worse, so she supposed she should count her blessings. She looked around the decrepit room, dust and cobwebs covered everything, along with that slight scent of mold that abandoned houses could get.

Her feet crunched through the detritus as she entered the room, her eyes noticed the bookshelf on the far side of the room. Ancient tomes, manuscripts, invaluable works of literature, sitting here rotting on the shelves. Marie lightly ran her fingers across the spines, part of her aching to save them from their doom, the other knowing she was running out of time.

"Bellissimo, wouldn't you say? This one holds a special secret." The driver said as he pointed to a small book, different than the others. 'Sneewittchen' the title read, Marie drew in a breath.

"A Grimm brothers original, it seems." She reached for the book, but it wouldn't budge, save tilting slightly forward. Beside her the bookcase began to swing forward, the rust on the mechanics making them protest loudly. Marie glanced at the driver suspiciously. "And how did you know of this?"

"I said it was trespassing, I never said I hadn't done it." He replied with a smirk, pulling a flashlight from his pocket, heading toward the staircase, descending into the darkness beyond the opening. Marie locked eyes with Dalil, something was all wrong about this, she could feel it. Everything in her screamed to leave and never return, but she had to know if the next piece of the key was beyond the secret entrance.

He was only human after all. What problems could he possibly present to her? She removed the spear from it's binding and followed the driver, her every sense alert to danger. The stench of disuse and the elements clouding the air as the staircase changed from modern building to ancient. The driver lit the torches around the room at the bottom of the staircase.

It was a masterpiece of architecture, the like she hadn't seen in hundreds of years, she marveled at the lost knowledge enabling them to keep out the moisture. Faded murals were painted on the walls, shelves of scrolls lined others. They had found the repository of vampire knowledge and lore, the tale of Ambrogio's change forever captured for all time on the walls. Marie picked up a scroll, it appeared to be stories of their history after Ambrogio had returned to the area.

A shimmering in the corner caught her attention. There, laying as it had for a millennia, was a skeleton, clothed in silver armor. Marie saw her family crest on the breast plate, was their journey at an end? Had her ancestor died before the keys had all been planted?

Behind her the door slammed and the driver let out a low chuckle. "She will reward me handsomely for you two. You're one of them." He scoffed, gesturing with his chin at the skeleton. "You would bring harm to the queen."

Marie cursed under her breath, of course, this fool was one of the misguided souls who pledged their life to a vampire, in hopes that they would be turned. Little did they know, it always ended in death for the human, they were never turned.

"She's using you." Marie warned him, as he pulled a pistol from his pocket.

"She promised to make me immortal, I bring her victims, when I have done enough, she will reward me."

"With death."

Doubt crossed his face for a moment, then he shook his head. "She will come. She has to this time." His eyes slightly wild as he spoke.

Marie stared at the ground, she hated this part, but they

couldn't wait to see if Lorelai would arrive. "Forgive me." She whispered as she raised the spear and threw it at him, the end piercing his chest. The gun fired, barely missing Dalil, the bullet lodging in the stone of the ancient walls, cracking the mural.

The life drained from his eyes as Marie turned to the skeleton, quickly removing the breast plate. She attempted to be careful with the bones of her ancestor, but they crumbled to dust as she lifted the silver plate. Dalil coughed as the dust floated about the room, then pointed to the inside of the armor. Marie gently turned it over, revealing writing engraved into the metal.

'My ancestor, I have chosen to
be the one to sacrifice my life
to bring you here. The knowledge
found in this room will be
invaluable in your quest. I
only pray I make it to my
destination before they destroy
me. Take the knowledge you find
and this key and take them to
Ohanna. Only then will you
learn how to defeat Selene
for all time.'

Next to the script, was another piece of the key hooked to the armor. Marie pulled it free as she looked at the bookshelf. "Grab as many as you can. We must leave, he may have actually warned them." Dalil nodded as he filled his arms with the precious scrolls and walked past the body of the driver without a second glance.

Marie retrieved her spear, turning the handle at the bottom of the stairs to open the door, at least this one wasn't hidden. She looked at the shelves, still filled with priceless knowledge, praying the scrolls they would be able to save would give them the answers they needed. They couldn't save them all or they risked being caught.

Marie grabbed the reins of the horses as they climbed into the carriage and urged them away from the manor. They needed to return to Alexandria and fast.

CHAPTER THIRTY ONE

Lorelai rolled her eyes as she noticed the light glowing on the wall. The map alerted her to trespassing in the different nests and important locations around the world. She dropped the body she was feeding on and groaned, Venice, it was that ridiculous tour guide again. He had been insistent on being turned, he had provided a few nice meals when she had been in the area, but she grew weary of him rapidly.

It was time to destroy that piece of their past and the evil that lay within. She shuddered every time she thought of the hunter that lay entombed within that manor, who had come close to ending her life. She knew that one knew too much, Lorelai needed to bury her along with the other pieces of the past. Only the future mattered now.

She turned angrily from the map and back to her guests. She would not let that fool ruin her evening. So he had lured a few victims? She had more than enough here. Once she had put the next part of her plan in motion, she would take a quick trip to Venice to give him his eternal reward.

"Is everything alright, my queen." One of her minions questioned, noting her annoyance as well as the flashing on the map.

"It's fine. We will deal with that later."

"Yes, my queen." He responded, his eyes glinting evilly, he hoped he would accompany her this time, he was tired of guarding the nest. He was ready for another to gain the 'honor'.

Lorelai mingled with the members of her coven, but the room suddenly seemed empty to her. So many still slept, waiting for the precious blood that would awaken them. Her plan had begun, she enjoyed taking this human celebration and making it one of their own.

Tonight they gave thanks, soon they would give a present to the world, and by the time the ball dropped on the new year, Lorelai planned to be firmly cemented as the queen of the world, not just one country, the entire world. Once she awakened this nest, she would travel the world to waken the others.

The human cattle she had tended for so long would be lost without her guidance, after all, she had been behind the scenes for so long. Turning and guiding important figures of history, to ensure that her kind survived, that humans flourished, so when the time was right, her people would never know hunger or want again. It had been a long road, one full of sacrifice, but it would all be worth it once her plan was complete.

All she needed now was to destroy the hunter that still survived, the last of her kind. Lorelai had followed Ohanna's children, hunting them, killing those she could. But Ohanna had been so clever in hiding them. They were like ghosts, coming and going, striking without warning, as the centuries passed, Ohanna's children had passed down the knowledge of how to hurt and kill vampires.

But they were only human and so easy to break once they were caught. Even the one in Venice had crumpled quickly, if it hadn't been for that damn armor... Lorelai pushed the unhappy thoughts from her mind and plastered a smile on her face.

Tonight she would celebrate, tomorrow she would burn the ties to the past, as she had done so many times.

CHAPTER THIRTY TWO

The return trip to Alexandria was a blur to Marie, as she was lost in the memories of Venice. She couldn't get the vision of her dead ancestor out of her head, the armor sparkled in her minds eye. Should she have taken it? It was hard enough to transport the items they had, without adding the large silver armor, but Marie felt she may live to regret this in the future. She was going into her final battle, that may have been the difference between winning and losing.

Roger had already arranged for transportation of the spear and scrolls to his office at Alexandria. Marie worried as the lid to the box was sealed and loaded onto the plane. All their hope rested in that box, the script had said there were important answers in that room. She prayed they had grabbed the proper scrolls.

As the plane took off, Marie turned the pieces of the key over and over in her hands. They did not yet have the completed key, now she was told to take them to Ohanna? Where was Ohanna? The last mention of her in the scrolls was in Athens, but they had already been to Athens and been directed elsewhere. Ohanna couldn't still be alive, could she?

The plane shook as it hit some minor turbulence. Marie would get no answers here, she closed her eyes and fell into blessed sleep, brief as it may be on the short flight. Her dreams were clouded with images of her trip, always haunted by the eyes of Lorelai, always watching, always laughing as Marie struggled to reach her goal.

The wheels screeched as the plane touched down and Marie blinked the sleep from her eyes. Hopefully Roger would have found some answers on his end. They collected their luggage, then hurried to the car Roger had sent to pick them up, ensuring that the precious box was loaded into the trunk. Dalil sighed with relief as he rested his head on the seat back.

"That was most definitely an adventure, but I am happy to be back. I'm getting too old for this."

Marie nodded, not willing to speak more in the car, she didn't know the driver and wasn't willing to risk sharing anything that could compromise their quest. The car pulled up to Roger's office, Roger was waiting at the curb, excitement obvious on his face. He hurried them to his office, the box in tow. He closed the door, turning to Marie.

"Is it really it?" He asked looking at the box.

"The spear? Yes. I believe it is." Marie opened the box, she retrieved the spear, handing it to Roger, his hands shook as he took it from her. "Once I have defeated Lorelai, it is yours." She gestured to the scrolls that were nestled in the box. "All of this is yours. I want you to preserve it in the museum. That's where it all belongs."

Roger nodded somberly, placing the spear back in the box. "I swear, I will honor the legacy of your family to the best of my ability."

Dalil looked at them strangely. "Don't talk so morbidly, you sound like you don't believe you will survive this. We will find the answers to defeating her, then we will celebrate our victory together. All of us." Dalil said as he looked into her eyes, his hands gripping her shoulders, as if to reassure himself.

Marie and Roger exchanged a glance, exchanging knowledge that only they two shared. "Yes, of course." Marie responded absently. "Now we need to find the final piece." She pulled the key pieces from her pack, then placed them on Roger's desk, carefully placing them together until they created a small circle. "See? There is a piece that goes in the middle. The last clue said to take them to Ohanna, but we have no idea where she could be."

Roger looked at the pieces, the silver glowing softly in the lamp light. "I may have an idea. Bring your baton." He said as he picked up the pieces, walking to the door.

"Where are we going?" Marie called after him as he ran to his car. Marie hadn't seen Roger this excited in years, he was even more excited than he was at the reveal of the spear.

"While you two have been busy tromping through Europe, I have been searching for any clues I can find as to the location of the tomb. I kept returning to the stone time and time again, hoping we missed some small detail or clue, and I believe we did, but I must show you." The companions remained silent for the rest of the trip as Roger weaved in and out of traffic.

The car had barely stopped, when Roger flung open the door, hurrying through the ruins to the stone with the first clue. "Open it quickly please, I must see if my recollection is correct."

Marie inserted the baton to open the hidden panel, once again revealing the first clue. "Go back to where it all began. We did that, there is nothing else here."

"But there is. Look." Roger pointed to a shallow recess at the bottom of the panel, a small circle, exactly like the key pieces. "I didn't really think of it when we came here the first time, and the panel has been closed since, but seeing the pieces on my desk jogged the memory. Insert them and see what happens."

Marie took the pieces from Roger, quickly inserting them into the hole. "They fit perfectly, but there must be more to it."

"There always is." Laughed Dalil, looking carefully at the stone. He reached out and pressed on the pieces, they slid into the stone a bit farther and a soft click was heard. The panel slid down, revealing another clue.

You have done well. To find
Ohanna you must search the
Library.

Rolled up below the inscription, was a map of the great

Library of Alexandria.

CHAPTER THIRTY THREE

"It makes no sense. I have seen every diagram of the Library that we have, and I have never seen this chamber before. How could it have gone unnoticed?"

"Perhaps it was meant to." Dalil mumbled.

"What do you mean?"

"We have seen how the ancestors of Ohanna created the Tomb, the series of key pieces, and the journey to find them. Perhaps this goes back farther than that. What was here before the Library? Ohanna lived more than 1000 years before we believe the Library was built, perhaps she was entombed there, then later, the Library was built over her. Perhaps her ancestors carried the secret of where her tomb lie, they helped build the Library, adding the knowledge of the secret room to this single map."

"That's a lot of ifs and a bit of a stretch."

"Because all of this is so logical?" Dalil raised his eyebrow. "We have traveled to the literal Underworld in search of a way to kill the Queen of the Vampires, while following in the footsteps of the first vampire ever created, and you say my theory is a stretch?"

"I concede to your point." Roger grabbed a leather bag from behind his desk. "This time, I refuse to stay behind."

"It could be dangerous."

"I'm ready."

The trio walked to the door, Roger froze with his hand on the door handle as Marie questioned him. "No one knows where the Library was, that knowledge was lost to time."

"My entire career has been dedicated to discovering the past secrets of Egypt, Cleopatra's palace, the Library at Alexandria, both were supposed to have been lost to the sea. But why? For decades, I have poured over every document, learning anything I could as to the whereabouts of the Library. Hoping perhaps one day, I could find where it sank and discover it. I believe that I have found the location it was originally at, though I had no reason to begin an excavation. Now, we do."

"Well, you do have ground penetrating radar, but surely something has been built there by now."

"Let's find out." They drove to the East Harbor, the sun sparkled on the water as the ships moved about the bay. "This was once the ancient Port of Alexandria. Here stood the great Pharos Lighthouse and the Library. At some point in history, the water flooded the land and submerged the ruins of the lighthouse, many say the Library as well, but I believe they are wrong. According to the text Dalil showed us, the library was destroyed by a woman of great evil, I believe that was either Selene or Lorelai. We do not know when Lorelai was created, but if Dalil's theory is correct, perhaps one of them destroyed the Library in order to find the resting place of Ohanna and the knowledge within. She could have discovered that the Tomb had been created and thought the key lie with Ohanna. I believe she attacked the Library multiple times, then eventually obliterated it completely in her search for Ohanna."

"But where is the secret room?"

Roger stopped the car at the edge of the harbor, the ground here slightly higher than the rest. "From the documents and stories I have read, I believe the lighthouse was out there, and the Library would have been here." They all looked around the space, the raised portion of the coastline was large enough for the building. Now, only some rocks and a few sad, empty buildings remained.

"Why are these buildings abandoned?"

"I don't know." They walked to the larger building. There

was a warning written on the door in Arabic, then repeated in a few other local languages. 'Do not enter. This building houses great evil. Save yourself.'

"Well that's inviting." Marie exclaimed as she pushed the door, it resisted, so she kicked in the crumbling wood. It was a simple housing unit, made with multiple rooms, most likely rooms for rent. "It seems normal to me." She said as she continued into the room, noting a small staircase in the back of the room leading down. "Down we go then." Marie looked down the staircase, the darkness ominous after the warning, she was glad she had remembered to grab the spear before they left Roger's office.

Dalil turned on his flashlight and illuminated the stairs ahead of her. It appeared that whoever owned the building had been doing some expanding, the walls were carved smooth in this part of the ground, the moisture from the bay evident in the strata.

"Not the best place for an expansion. The rooms would be moist." Dalil looked ahead, seeing the smooth walls change to rough digging, a dark hole was in the wall at the end of the tunnel. "What's this now?" He shown his light into the hole, revealing a stone door, inscribed in Greek, Ancient Egyptian and Arabic. 'Death will befall you.'

"I see why no one wants to live in the building now."

"Wait, there's more." Marie grabbed a pick from the ground near the hole where the workers had dropped it to remove more of the dirt. 'Vampires, Death will befall you.' was revealed. "I believe we have found the secret room and resting place of Ohanna." The two men helped remove the rest of the rock and dirt from the door.

"Look." Roger pointed to more of the inscription that had been revealed. 'Any creature with even one drop of vampire blood will die upon entering this chamber'.

CHAPTER THIRTY FOUR

Marie looked at the door, no lock with the family crest, this door was built prior to the key pieces and the quest. Were they at the correct location? The warning was specifically to vampires, it had to be the right spot. Marie inspected the door and found a latch, it resisted, but finally the door slowly swung in. Marie took a step forward, but Roger grabbed her arm and hissed in her ear.

"You can't go in there. Did you read the warning?"

"I'll be fine. The potion distilled it, it was no longer blood."

Roger looked at her doubtfully but released her arm. Marie stepped through the door, pain, like fire spread through her body and she doubled over. "Ahh." She cried out.

"Allison!" Dalil shouted as Roger pulled her back through the door. "What happened? Why are you in pain?"

Marie laughed weakly. "I.. I stubbed my toe. It's nothing." She began to get up, but Roger held her tight. "Roger, I have to see her." She shrugged off his arm, then stood at the entryway again, this time prepared for the pain.

Inside the room glowed with a light of its own, some forgotten science, or perhaps a remnant of the magic of the old gods. In the center of the room, stood a glass box, containing an old woman. She appeared to be sleeping, as if Marie could lift the lid and she would awaken. For thousands of years, she had lay here perfectly preserved.

Marie struggled to put one foot in front of the other as

she made her way to Ohanna, she gasped as she looked upon the face of her ancestor. She looked so like her grandmother, for a moment the overwhelming pain of loss took her and tears began to fall.

"She is beautiful." Dalil said from beside her, gently placing his hand on hers in comfort, noticing the slight sheen of sweat on her brow. "Look." On a chain, around her neck lay the final piece of the key. They gently lifted the lid, no odor of embalming reached them, causing them to both wonder at the magic that lay within this body.

Finally, they had the final piece of the key, but they were no closer to the location of the Tomb. Roger wandered the edge of the room, his eyes riveted on the walls, but Marie's vision swam and blurred. Her breath began coming in short spurts. Her legs gave out and she fell to the floor, only saved by Dalil scooping her into his arms.

As he walked her from the room, her eyes fluttered back into her head. "I'm taking her up top, Roger, it seems the stale air has overcome her." Roger nodded as he continued to study the wall, taking pictures as he went. Dalil carried Marie up the stairs, he struggled, it had been long since he carried a woman anywhere.

Marie groaned as the fresh air hit her face. "Roger?" She moaned.

"No, my dear, just me. You gave me a fright, but I'll admit the air made me a little light headed as well."

"Yes, the air."

Roger hurried from the building, phone in hand, ready to show what treasure he had found.

"It seems we were left more than one message here." He scrolled to the first picture. "These are from Ohanna herself." He scrolled past a few pictures. "While these were written much later and seem to be part of our quest."

Marie reached for the phone weakly. Scrolling through the pictures.

'I lie here in this tomb,
my final gift from the
god Apollo, my sanctuary
from those who have pursued
me my entire life. Only my
children know of this room,
I have sent my four children
to the four directions. Only
one stays with me now to
carve you this message.
Take the knowledge
found in this tomb and
use it to destroy Selene
and her kind. The world
will never be safe while
she lives. I cannot ask
this of my own children,
they are known to her
and hunted mercilessly.
So I have sent them from
me with instructions to
hide, to teach their
children the lessons I
have taught them and
grow our family until
we are strong enough to
fight her. I pray, my child,
that you now come with
the strength to do this.'

Marie read the message multiple times, what knowledge? What had Ohanna left behind?

"There's more." Roger urged, scrolling to the next set of pictures.

'Ancestor, forgive me, I

have taken the knowledge
from this room and moved
it to a safer location.
Selene will stop at nothing
to enter this chamber, but
I dare not do more than
carve this message, I fear
to destroy the magic that
protects her and I will
not desecrate her tomb.
You have the map, you
have the key. You have
everything you need to
find the Tomb of the
Serapeum.'

Marie pulled the pieces of the key from her pocket and put them together. She turned the completed key over in her hands.

"The map." She whispered.

CHAPTER THIRTY FIVE

Lorelai rose with the moon, she was satisfied at the success of her party the night before. The only smudge on the joy of the evening was that damn light. She opened the dark curtains, looking into the dark, clear night. A soft blanket of snow covered the ground, sparkling in the moonlight. To the casual observer, her farm was out of a holiday movie, little did they know the danger that lurked within.

Her followers still slumbered below, drunk from overfeeding on the humans they had captured. Lorelai would let them rest, it was time to collect more sacrifices and wake the rest of the nest, but they had time. She sat in the plush chair and turned on the TV. She wondered what the humans would think if they knew their favorite pastime was created by the vampires as a way to monitor the humans and pass the time during the long summer days, when they could no longer slumber.

The news flashed across the screen, an older police officer was giving a report on the tragic accident that had happened at a nearby town, the entire town had been destroyed and all of the residents killed. The police were still investigating the freak accident that had ignited the gas lines beneath the city.

Behind the officer, slightly out of view, someone was trying to get his attention. Lorelai leaned in closer, she could read his lips as he yelled at the officer. "Vampires." She read as his lips moved, inaudible. She watched as the man struggled against the crowd, getting pulled away from the camera as other officers came forward.

She suddenly felt a sense of unease, it was too easy, too quiet. Where was the Huntress? Why had she allowed her to wreak havoc on that town? She had always been close at hand before. Lorelai knew she couldn't be dead, her wounds weren't that bad, so where had she disappeared to?

Lorelai knew the man she had just seen was their unwelcome visitor in the town. What had happened to Nikolai and the grandmother? Surely he hadn't killed them, but Nikolai had never failed her before. Perhaps this one was stronger than she had given him credit for. Her eyes narrowed as she played back the scene again, freezing the image as he came into view. Perhaps he would be a good candidate to join her coven, if he survived.

Lorelai rose gracefully, she dressed quickly, packing a small travel bag with a few changes of clothes. It was time to destroy the past and prepare for the future, there was too much hidden in Italy to leave it to chance. She slowly descended the staircase, the sounds of her followers waking and milling about reached her ears.

"Liam?" She called to one of her coven.

"Yes, my queen."

"We are taking a trip to Italy, I trust you can get me there quickly?"

"Of course, wheels up in 30."

Lorelai didn't know where he got the vehicles he obtained, nor did she care, he was an accomplished pilot, and her only choice for a driver that wasn't herself.

True to his word, in less than 30 minutes, a smaller private jet taxied down the long road to the farmhouse. "Welcome aboard, my queen." He held out a hand to assist her up the stairs, then settled her into a comfortable seat. "The takeoff may be a little bumpy, this bird wasn't made to take off on a road."

"When we have succeeded, you may have any airport you wish." Lorelai promised. Liam smiled and bowed, then walked back to the cockpit.

"We will be making a stop for fuel along the way, but it should be a smooth flight. Enjoy your flight, and your in flight meal." He opened a door to reveal the previous pilot tied up and struggling.

"Thank you, I'll save that for later." Lorelai licked her lips as Liam shut the door again, the sounds from the pilot now more frantic.

Lorelai relaxed as she watched the night fly by the window, she knew their arrival would be close to dawn, but she had faith he had already arranged a safe route. As they made their stop for fuel, Liam returned to pull the blinds on the windows.

"We will resume our flight at sundown, my queen, may I get you a blanket?"

"Yes please, and a snack before bed."

Liam walked to the cabinet, pulling the struggling pilot from within, the smell of his soiled pants filled the cabin. Lorelai drank her fill then offered the rest to Liam.

"Make sure that doesn't join us on the rest of our trip." Lorelai said, wrinkling her nose at the stench. As the sun set, the plane flew into the distance, the drained body of the pilot watching with empty eyes as it soared into the sky.

CHAPTER THIRTY SIX

Marie looked again at the carving in her hand, then returned to the map of the harbor, they had spread across Roger's desk, they had been at this all night, now the morning light filtered through the blinds. "This matches here and here, but this is different. Then there's this spot over here," she pointed to an area on the opposite side of the harbor, "it matches here but not here. We're running out of time." She slammed her hand down on the table in frustration.

"This is a modern map, do you have anything older? Before so much construction was done?"

Roger looked sadly at Dalil. "Nothing this old." He said, gesturing to the key.

"Anything would help."

Roger pulled out a box of old maps and began to carefully leaf through them. "These are all I have of the area." He pulled out a small stack of maps, all from different time periods and placed them on the table. Dalil looked at them carefully from oldest to youngest.

"Of course our modern map is most accurate, due to our technology, but the key wasn't made by technology, it was made by human hands." He looked at the oldest map, then was silent for a moment. "Can we scan the key to enlarge the image?"

"Of course, what's on your mind?" Roger said as he hurried to the computer, offering him the image a few moments later.

"The map on the key is rather vague, more elevation lines of the bottom of the harbor than landmarks, but if we assume this dot is the ancient lighthouse, perhaps we can discover our location."

Marie pulled out a light table, turning it on so they would be able to overlay the images, then helped move the map and image into place.

"Look," she said pointing to a small area on the map, "it's there. It has to be." Her eyes were excited as she looked from Dalil to Roger.

"I have a boat and diving equipment ready. Let the adventure continue." Roger laughed as they headed to the door.

The waters were calm as the boat set sail, plotting a course for an area in the middle of the harbor. Marie and Dalil struggled into the wetsuits and tanks for the dive, Roger would stay up top to ensure their safety as the harbor was still an active port.

"The harbor is generally shallow, but you can see there are a few deeper areas around where we believe the Tomb to be. You will be able to communicate via your headsets, and remember, that Tomb has been closed for centuries, it will be dangerous and the air will be toxic. Be safe, both of you." He urged while looking into Marie's eyes. "Move slowly, as there can be sharks."

Marie and Dalil nodded, then headed to the platform to begin their dive. Marie turned on the transponder, so Roger could track their location, then she adjusted her helmet and sunk beneath the waves.

"Roger, Dalil, can you hear me?" Her voice crackled across the speaker.

"Loud and clear, my dear. Dalil is joining you now." Soon the older man was drifting down through the water to join her as she floated, waiting and observing the water around her.

"There's more fauna here than I expected." Dalil quipped as he looked around nervously.

"Let's descend. Roger, keep us on course." Marie began swimming toward the sea floor, her eyes constantly scanning the surrounding waters.

"Adjust your course slightly left." Roger's voice said in their ears. As they dove deeper, they could see various columns and artifacts from the ancient world.

"The Library?" Dalil wondered aloud.

"Perhaps, but that is not our quest. We have more important things to worry about. Roger mark this spot, perhaps we can return another time."

"Roger that." Roger laughed.

They swam along the sea floor, careful to not stir the silt along the bottom.

"How close are we?"

"You should be there."

Marie looked around the area, it looked as if a landslide had occurred here. Her heart sunk, what if the Tomb was covered? How would they reach it now? They were so close. She heard Dalil gasp as a shark swum close.

"Easy, my friend. He's just curious." She began to lower herself to the floor, Dalil did the same, waiting for the beast to circle the area and swim away.

"Whew, I was not expecting that." Dalil laughed. Once this adventure is over, I'm retiring to my old arm chair, so I can enjoy my pipe and my books."

"As well you should." Marie smiled back, looking fondly at her new friend, a dark ravine behind him catching her attention.

"What is it?" Dalil asked as she stared past him.

"Maybe nothing, maybe everything." Marie slowly swam forward, inching into the dark crevasse. Silt drifted down on her from above, she turned on her light to see the path ahead. At the end of the dark space, the wall seemed different. Marie ran her hands over the walls, silt making the water murky.

For a moment she couldn't see the wall, but as her hand moved again, she felt a small hole. She stilled her hand, allowing the water to clear, her breath catching in her throat. The keyhole. At last they had found the Tomb of the Serapeum.

CHAPTER THIRTY SEVEN

Marie could vaguely feel Dalil's hand on her shoulder as she removed the key from her pouch, her hands were shaking and she almost dropped it, but his steadying hands were there to catch it. Together they lifted the key to the hole.

"It doesn't turn... maybe we should push." They pushed on the small key, the silt in the keyhole making it difficult, so they tried again.

"No use." They pulled the key out, they could see the years under the sea had filled the hole enough that it wouldn't work.

"I have an idea." She pulled a small brush from her wetsuit, then began to painstakingly clean the silt from the keyhole. "I had a feeling we'd need it." They inserted the key again and pushed, this time the key gave way, slipping into the wall. The opening shifted into the wall, releasing a cloud of silt into the water.

Dalil reached for Marie so they wouldn't lose each other in the murk and they moved into the darkness. "I can't see anything."

"Neither can I, but it looks like the path goes up? I swear I see light ahead."

"I do too. What could still be lit after all this time?"

"Much knowledge was lost when the Library was destroyed, knowledge that was used to build this Tomb." Slowly they moved forward toward the dim light, their breath shallow and halting as their heads broke the surface and entered the entrance to the Tomb. Ahead of them was a long tunnel, at the end, they could see a room lit by an unknown source.

"Ok you two, time to come back, your tanks are getting low. We know where it is, you can go back down to explore after you change out and rest a moment." Roger warned them.

"Just a moment, I want to see the room, then we will surface."

"Ma.. Allison! Don't take risks. You have a partner to think about."

Marie looked at Dalil and he nodded his head. "Five minutes, then we'll be up." Roger grumbled again, but stayed silent. The duo moved forward into the room. "Oh Roger, I wish you could see this." Marie breathed as the full splendor of the room was revealed.

Murals covered the walls, telling the history of her family since the day Ohanna had died, and in the center of the room was a large, glittering sword.

"I expect pictures." Roger reminded her as she moved forward to record the precious fresco.

"The Sun Sword." Marie read softly as she examined the sword. "According to this, The Sun Sword was given to my family, by the god Apollo himself, as a way to kill Selene. It is the only weapon that can kill a god, or goddess, as the case may be. All of the weapons my family used had slivers of this sword forged into them, that's why none of the weapons I made myself worked! This is it Dalil! This is what we were searching for." Marie heard a sound off to her left, a low growl and a thud. "Dalil?"

Marie turned, Dalil stared into the darkness of another tunnel. The sound was heard again. Marie looked closer, she saw the reflection of eyes moving toward them. "Dalil, get behind me."

"No, I'll protect you, grab the sword and go."

"Get back!" Marie ordered, turning to face him. She heard the creature move, but when she turned back it was gone. "Where is it? Get out of here Dalil!" Marie reached for the sword, she had to get it, this was their only chance.

"Ahh." Marie heard Dalil cry, as she turned she saw the creature grab him and rip at his diving equipment, tearing the hose, allowing the toxic air of the Tomb to enter his suit.

"Dalil. Don't breathe." Marie lunged herself into the creature knocking it off balance, forcing it to drop Dalil. "Take mine." Marie ripped the helmet from her head, dropping her tanks as the creature regained its footing. It was a vampire, old and feral, it had been trapped here alone and starving for centuries, it's curse that it would never die of that gnawing hunger.

"Allison." Dalil gasped.

"Put. It. On." Marie could feel the poisonous air burn her lungs, but like the vampire, it couldn't kill her. She placed herself between the demon and Dalil, listening as he slowly replaced his helmet with hers. She knew they didn't have much time until the air ran out and he would be lost.

Marie tested the weight of the sword in her hand, perfectly balanced, it felt good to hold a proper weapon once again. The demon circled them, testing her, his eyes on his prey, knowing the old man was the easier meal. His eyes were wild as he rushed forward, starvation making him sloppy.

Marie swung the sword connecting with his outstretched arm, severing it from the body. Madness filled the creature as he turned on Marie, grabbing her, slamming them both into the wall. Marie could hear it crack as their combined weight tested the ancient structure.

"Go to the door! I'll be right behind you." She called as the monster slammed her into the wall again, a crack appearing behind her head. Marie shoved against him with all her strength, his rage making him strong, but his emaciation worked against him, he wasn't strong enough.

Marie shoved him away, stabbing him through the heart, a squeal of rage filled the Tomb as she pulled the sword out, then chopped off his head. The room began to crumble as Marie ran to the exit, grabbing a stunned Dalil, swimming through the doorway as the Tomb collapsed, and the priceless fresco was destroyed.

Marie pushed off the seafloor as she swam as fast as she could to the surface. Her lungs burned, she could see Dalil was low on air as well. They burst through the surface, not far from the boat. Roger and the crew pulled them to safety.

"Oxygen." Roger called. Marie's vision swam at the lack of air, she sucked greedily as a mask was put to her face.

"It seems you have some explaining to do." Dalil said before passing out.

CHAPTER THIRTY EIGHT

1407 BC

Selene seethed as she watched from her new home. How dare they banish her to the moon? Ambrogio had broken all their laws, gone back on agreements with gods, and yet he was allowed to stay on the earth and play with his new creations, while she stayed here, alone and cold.

She watched as her once friend, Ohanna, stole away with her precious love notes and tried to show others how to destroy her love. She laughed when they turned her away, the fools that they were, only brought about their own destruction faster. As Ohanna traveled to seek the aid of Athena, Selene whispered into the night, aiding those who pursued her.

Rage filled Selene as she could only watch helplessly as Ohanna and her lover destroyed the children of Ambrogio, she screamed into the darkness, part of her soul dying with every stoke of the sword or spear. Selene remembered Artemis's words, she could choose to return to the earth, but she would lose her soul.

So she bided her time, a spy for Ambrogio and his children, the darkness was never safe for Ohanna and her family. They learned to hide well, even on the rare days that the moon traveled across the daytime sky. But Selene was cunning as well, she watched and waited, when Ohanna was finally at the end of her life, Selene rejoiced, finally her love would be safe, finally she could join him without fear.

But alas, that was not to be true. Apollo was too wise, he could feel her desires and the one god whose favor she had once held, turned on her. He granted The Sun Sword to Ohanna, he showed her how to make weapons from it to destroy her and any she would create from her goddess blood.

Slowly, over the centuries, her love turned to hate, she realized the curse of the moon was actually a choice. She could choose to return and lose her soul in an instant, or she could stay here and have it wither and die over time, in agonizing pain.

Selene knew that Ohanna's children were long since dust, but her ilk remained. Her children had multiplied, they had taught their children and grandchildren how to hunt the vampires. Selene followed them all, she found their weapons of evil, and she planned. She would leave the moon, she would sacrifice her soul, and she would destroy the hunters. The earth would be their playground, and the humans who remained would be their food.

Selene, the Goddess of the Moon, descended in a fiery ball, that crashed to the earth in a massive explosion. She wrought her wrath on any human who dared to stand against her, and then they came. The children of Ohanna, with their weapons of Apollo, that burned like the sun.

They fought her back, she knew she was not strong enough to defy their weapons. She needed to create more like her. With her new followers, she attacked their cities and destroyed their repositories of knowledge, burning them to the ground and killing or turning the scholars.

Selene knew that Ohanna's tomb held the one weapon that could destroy her, so she found Ohanna's tomb, set on destroying the weapon once and for all. But magic surrounded the tomb, stopping any of vampire blood from entering. Selene paced, just outside the open door, seething as she watched Ohanna, laying in her casket, peaceful, she appeared only to be asleep.

Selene screamed in rage and the walls of the tomb shook, if she couldn't destroy the sword, then she would make sure no one ever found it. She ordered her followers to bury the tomb and destroy any marker of the grave. It was time to put her plan into action. She traveled to the homeland of Ambrogio, there she found his new coven.

She needed no invitation, she was their Queen. She pushed the doors, they flew off their hinges, startling those inside.

"Hello, my love." She smiled evilly.

CHAPTER THIRTY NINE

The wheels screeched loudly as the plane touched down, Lorelai descended the stairs like the Queen she was, and no one, not even the airport security questioned their unannounced arrival. She slipped on her sunglasses, even though it was dark, another hint at those around her, to leave her alone.

Liam taxied away as she slowly walked to the front of the airport, she knew he would find her with another form of transportation. As expected, he soon pulled up in a fancy red sports car, the top down, the evening breeze ruffling his hair. He hurried around the car, opening the door for her. "My Queen, will there be any stops you require or straight to our destination?"

"Straight on through."

The tires squealed as he pulled away from the curb and into the night. The wind whipped her hair around her stormy face. Her unease continued to grow, something was wrong, the Huntress was up to something.

The beauty of Venice was ignored by the pair as they drove to the mansion, the home of the original coven of their kind. Lorelai wrinkled her nose at the decrepit building, she should have done this long ago. Memories of her last visit to this place washed over her, she shook her head to banish them from her thoughts.

'That's odd.' She thought to herself. 'The door is open. That fool must have forgotten.' She moved across the rickety floor with a rare grace, standing in the open doorway. The room was dark but she could see perfectly, the door to the nest was open as well. Was he giving tours?

Lorelai looked out the door, no carriage. When she found him, she would make sure he suffered for this disrespect. It didn't matter to her that she planned on destroying everything within the building, all that mattered was that the human offended her and disrespected their ancient home. It was bad enough he used them to make money, but at least he could close things up when he left.

She crossed the room in a few angry strides, the smell of blood wafting up the stairs, making her mouth water slightly. Why would there be blood? The fool hadn't been turned, was he pretending now? Lorelai rolled her eyes, the lengths that man would go to.

She descended the staircase, a single torch fluttered below, barely lit, threatening to go out. At the base of the stairs she saw a crumpled form, what was this? The scent of blood was heavier now, she could hear Liam growl behind her, the scent affecting him more than her.

"What?" She looked at the body, recognizing the face of the tour guide, she looked around the room. "No!" The shelves were missing scrolls, pieces of their history. "No!" She glanced at the body of the armored hunter, she saw the armor had been removed, the body crumbled. She hurried forward, noticing the writing inside. They had been plotting against her in secret all these years, hiding clues, helping a successor in her destruction. Lorelai took a deep breath, her, she smelled her, the Huntress had been here, and another, one she didn't know, yet.

"NOOOO!" She screamed as she realized all her carefully laid plans were crashing down. A pain, like ice, pierced her chest, she looked down. Nothing, only shocking pain. She touched her hand to her breast as the pain continued to spread. One of her children had been murdered. She could feel it.

"We go, take me to Ohanna, I don't care how you do it, but get me there NOW!" Liam shuddered as Lorelai stormed past him. As they returned to the airport, police were already examining their aircraft. In her rage, she killed them all, uncaring as to the crowd that cowered at the edge of the runway. Let them see, let them all see. She would destroy them all.

The trip to Alexandria was a red blur of rage. As Lorelai descended the earthen stairs to the entrance of the tomb, her breath froze. The door was open, Ohanna slept in her casket as peaceful as ever, and the sword was gone. The Huntress had the sword.

CHAPTER FORTY

Dalil groaned as he sat up, his head hurt from his diving experience. "That's it, I want my armchair and my books."

"What? No pipe?" Marie teased, as he looked at her steadily.

"As I said before, you have some explaining to do." Marie looked down, she took a deep breath, ready to begin her tale. "However, so do I. I feel it's only fair that I tell you my tale before you tell me yours." Marie nodded her head, she sat back, waiting for him to explain. Dalil sighed, long and low.

"I'm not even sure where to begin. This journey we have been on, the quest left by your family, it was not left for you alone. It was left for me as well." Marie's eyes shot to Dalil's face as he continued.

"Ohanna sent four of her children to the four directions as is written in her tomb, but you didn't read it correctly, the one who stayed behind was not the fourth child, but the fifth child, the keeper of the knowledge. The one child who was not taught to fight, rather they were taught above all to hide and preserve the families knowledge so it would never be lost to time.

That child alone knew the locations of the others, that child was sworn to secrecy, all knowledge of it was hidden from all except the immediate family. For all intents and purposes, that child was a ghost."

Roger sat down heavily next to Marie. "So all this time, you've known about," he waved his hand to indicate the city, "all of this."

"I had knowledge, but like anything, some was unfortunately lost to time. My lineage helped the others along the way, granting them knowledge when they had lost some, never telling them who they were."

He looked at Marie. "I knew your lineage the moment I set eyes on you, cousin. You look so much like your ancestor that my grandmother befriended." Marie had a soft smile on her face at the memory of her friend.

"Well, it seems your ancestors didn't have all the knowledge, or one chose not to pass it along." Marie closed her eyes, nervous for once, Roger made sure none of the crew were in earshot. "My name is Marie Chasseur, I was born somewhere around the year 1130 AD, my mother was killed when I was very young, I was raised by my grandmother. She taught me nothing of vampire hunting, I didn't even know of their real existence until the day she was killed by their Queen in front of me. I thought all of her stories were just that... stories. How wrong I was."

Marie stopped, the painful memories too much. Dalil patted her hand, his light touch giving her the strength to continue.

"My husband and my grandmother died at her hand, that night I swore to avenge them. I took up her weapons and found a way to prolong my life." She looked up in shock. "The apothecary, he was one of your ancestors."

"It is possible, but I have no knowledge of this part of the tale."

"Perhaps like the fifth child, he felt it best to hide this knowledge." Dalil nodded at her words as she continued. "We created a potion to make me immortal, but not turn into the bloodthirsty creature she and her kind are."

"Now I understand your distress at Ohanna's Tomb."

"Yes, I chose to end my mortal life, to begin an eternal one as The Huntress. The woman your grandmother knew, was me. I loved her, she was the dearest friend I ever had, and Lorelai took her from me as well. Tell me though, how are you here? I thought Lorelai killed all of her children?"

Dalil shook his head sadly. "Not all, but almost. My father

was the only one to escape. She made him promise to run and never look back, to find you and keep you safe."

"And here we are. Together." Marie took his hand and rested her forehead on his. "Family." She whispered as a tear slipped down her cheek.

CHAPTER FORTY ONE

Marie kicked off her shoes, massaging her feet as she sat next to the roaring fire in Roger's den. They had retreated to his home for the evening, to compile all of their findings and plan their next move. Marie knew that Lorelai would be suspicious of her absence, perhaps she was even looking for her by now.

Her feet ached so badly after all the travel and adventure, this one scar that Lorelai had left upon her body that never healed, she could always feel the burning.

"Are you alright my dear?" Dalil questioned, concern evident upon his face.

"Yes, of course," she replied, hiding her mutilated feet under the throw, "just weary from all the adventure."

"As am I. When this is over, I will invite you to my family home... our family, we shall relax and enjoy the warm days in the sun, no cares in the world."

"Of course." Marie responded, but he didn't hear her, his soft snoring was all that greeted her. Marie smiled gently, taking the throw from her feet and covering him, sitting down next to him, leaning into him for comfort. It was a beautiful thought, but one that would never come to fruition.

Marie drifted into slumber, her aching feet bringing back the memories of that awful night. The night she was captured and tortured by Lorelai for sport.

* * * *

1200 AD

Music filled the air as the full moon smiled down on the

gathering. Dresses swayed as guests twirled round the room to the music. Marie crept along the balcony, she had finally caught Lorelai off guard, hosting this large wedding for herself and whichever 'love' she had this week.

Silent as a shadow she moved down the hall to the bridal suite, Lorelai was inside, preparing herself for the ceremony. The door opened with but a breath of a creak, Marie paused, waiting to see if she had been detected. She released her breath, moving forward, ahead of her she could see the bride, primping in front of the mirror.

She rushed forward, weapon in hand and spun Lorelai around. The bride screamed as she saw the weapon, Marie dropped her hand, recognizing a girl from the village, terror plain on her face. Lorelai rushed into the room, guards on her heels.

"Seize her." She ordered as she hurried to the young woman. "Are you all right? Did she hurt you?" The woman shook her head, the shock still stealing her voice. "I told you she was evil, but you were so brave to offer to stand in for me so we could capture her."

"Of course, Princess. We cannot allow her evil to survive and threaten you any longer." The girl breathed. Marie was placed in shackles, then led into the main hall, the dancers paused as she was brought to the front and placed in a cage.

"Today," Lorelai announced to the crowd, "on the day of my wedding. We have finally caught the evil one, The Huntress, the one who has tormented me all this time."

"It's true," the young woman spoke up, "she tried to kill me." An angry murmur rippled through the crowd, Marie's heart sunk, Lorelai had turned them all against her, an evil Queen who only desired innocent Lorelai's death. Marie watched in silence as a masked man moved to the front of the hall next to the altar, waiting as Lorelai glided up the aisle to join him.

The words of their wedding ceremony were lost to her as she saw the triumph in Lorelai's eyes. She had won, Marie was captured, she would be tortured, unable to die, living eternity in misery. The cage was opened as a pair of white hot sandals were brought forward, the heat making them crackle and pop.

"No!" Marie cried out. "No, don't." She screamed as the guards grabbed her and held her down. "Noooooo." Tears streamed down her face as the sandals were strapped to her feet and she was thrown onto the dance floor. She jumped back and forth from foot to foot, attempting to relieve some of the pain, even just for a moment, but it was impossible.

Marie's head swam as she threatened to pass out, but a guard slapped her to attention. "You will dance for our Princess. Now dance!" Marie looked around the room, frantic to escape the burning. Across the room there was an open window, overlooking the cliffs to the sea. Marie 'danced' across the room, then threw herself from the window, Lorelai's enraged scream following her as she fell into the ocean below, sighing as the cool water quenched her feet.

* * * *

Marie was shaken awake, Roger and Dalil stood over her. "Wake up Marie."

"I'm awake."

"You were crying."

"It was just a dream, all just a very bad dream." She responded as she glanced at her scarred feet again.

CHAPTER FORTY TWO

"These scrolls are no help." Marie exclaimed as she dropped another useless scroll to the table. They had spread every artifact they had found on their trip across the large, wooden dinner table.

"This one mentions the return of Selene, but it appears there is a second scroll that we don't have." Roger sighed as he sat heavily in the cushioned chair. Marie took the scroll from him.

"So where is Selene? Was she killed? Is she still alive? Is that who made Lorelai?" Marie rubbed her hands over her face. She had the sword, but two vampire queens seemed to be a steep undertaking. Killing Lorelai but not defeating her predecessor would be fruitless, the ancient vampire would just create more. Marie had to strike at the heart of the coven, she needed to kill the first queen.

"When Selene began her path of destruction, much knowledge was lost. Our ancestors lost track of her, and Ambrogio, they must be alive though." Dalil murmured, absently stroking his lower lip.

"In all my years of hunting, I have never seen one more powerful than Lorelai. I had never even seen a vampire before the day she killed my family."

"Then they must be sleeping, waiting for Lorelai, as their general, to bring about their vampiric apocalypse."

Marie smiled wryly, all this time she had assumed Lorelai was the vampire Queen, and yet it seemed she was only the princess after all. This knowledge didn't make her feel better, even though she knew it must make Lorelai furious to not be the true leader. Vampires were tied together, Marie had learned over the years. You kill the one who made another and you killed them both.

It was a fatal flaw Marie could only imagine was done purposely by the gods, but that only meant the true queen would be guarded fiercely. Marie ran her hands over the sword, the metal had a slight warmth to it, unlike any she had felt before. Each vampire made by Selene would have a bit of her blood, her goddess blood, she knew the sword and the spear, like in Ohanna's first battle, would be the only weapons that would allow them to succeed.

"None of it matters." She told the men, pushing the scrolls away. "I must return, with the weapons, to New York, that is the last place I saw her. I can only hope to find her trail. She must have a nest there, it would only make sense to keep them near large cities, far enough away as to not draw attention, but near enough to hunt easily.

"You will not go alone." Dalil put his hand on her shoulder, grabbing the spear.

"We're coming with you. You can't do this alone."

Marie looked at the two older men, she couldn't sacrifice them in order to succeed, but they were right, she couldn't do this alone. "Come with me, help me find the nest, but when it comes time to face her, I go alone. I am the only one she can't kill, she would either kill you or turn you, as a way to hurt me. Please, don't make me watch you die." A tear slipped down her cheek as she spoke, the memory of her family intruding into her mind.

"We may be old, but we aren't that easy to kill either." Dalil winked at her, spinning the spear with ease and moving into a defensive position. "While my ancestor was not trained in battle and was only a keeper of knowledge, I saw how our family suffered and died at the hands of Lorelai and her kind. I learned some techniques of my own."

Marie nodded, she was touched at his desire to help, but even now she could see gaps in his defense. "We will speak more of this later, for now we need to return to America. I've been gone too long already."

Roger called the airline, making all the arrangements for them to travel, with the weapons, on the next flight to New York. As the twilight settled over the earth, Marie leaned back in her seat, ready for the long flight. The plane taxied onto the runway, preparing to take off. As they gained speed, the plane suddenly shuddered, screeching to a halt.

"Sorry about that folks." Came the pilot over the intercom. "It seems there is some confusion on the runway. We will be on our way in just a moment."

Marie looked out her window as a smaller plane taxied past them, preparing to cut them off and take their spot on the runway. The window screen lifted, Marie locked eyes with Lorelai. As the smaller plane lifted off and soared into the sky, Marie could see her angry face pressed against the window, her hands beating on the glass. The race to return was on.

CHAPTER FORTY THREE

The wheels screeched down on the runway as Marie hurried from her seat.

"Ma'am, you'll have to wait your turn, please remain seated until the plane is in the terminal." The haughty stewardess looked down her nose at Marie.

"I need to get off the plane, it's an emergency." Marie stood near the door, waiting for the plane to stop, she had completely forgotten about her carry on or even her companions in her rush to get to the artifacts. If Lorelai suspected she had the sword, she may attack the airport to retrieve it first.

"Ma'am, you need to sit down or I'll call security."

Dalil appeared next to Marie. "We don't have time to deal with them, sit down, everything will be fine." Roger was already on his cell phone, alerting the airport authorities of a possible plan to steal the artifacts.

"You're right, the sun is still up, we have time. I just wasn't prepared to see her when we did. She would have had to stop for a layover somewhere, unless they enthralled a human pilot." Marie apologized to the stewardess for creating the disturbance and returned to her seat, still fidgeting slightly. "We have time." She repeated to herself.

The stewardess eyed her wearily as she slowly released the passengers to disembark. For Marie, it seemed like time had stopped, but finally it was their turn. The trio made their way to airport security to retrieve the valuable boxes, an armed guard stood watching over them.

"Nothing out of the ordinary to report, sir. What's in the boxes?"

"Just some artifacts for a museum display. Priceless, of course, and on the radar of a black market group. I'd appreciate the utmost secrecy in this matter." Roger responded as he signed for the cargo. "By the way, has this plane arrived yet?" He handed the guard a note with the tail numbers from Lorelai's plane, the guard moved to a computer and typed them in.

"I'm sorry, this plane hasn't arrived, it isn't scheduled to at all, I don't see it in the system."

Roger took the paper from him. "My mistake, I must have written it down wrong." He exchanged a worried glance with Marie, there were dozens of airports she could have landed at, how would they find her now?

They loaded the crates into the vehicle Roger had arranged for them, quickly driving to the hotel, Marie sat with her hand on the boxes the entire ride. She wished she had a secure base of operations in New York, but she had long since stopped that practice. It was too easy for Lorelai to track her movements if she had locations to monitor.

They placed the accommodations under one of Marie's aliases, carefully checking the room, taking every precaution to ensure Lorelai hadn't discovered their plans. Roger turned on the tv randomly, to drown out any of their conversation from being overheard. They opened the crates and breathed a collective sigh of relief as they saw the glittering weapons, safe in their packaging.

An alert came on the television, blaring slightly and drawing their attention to the screen. "Manhattan police request everyone to stay inside and lock their doors. Suspect is armed and dangerous, last seen in the area between Times Square and Central Park." A grainy picture of Nikolai flashed across the screen.

"She's found me." Marie uttered, pulling the sword from the crate. "She's sent her hunter after me. Stay here, he's not far. Let no one in." Marie slipped out the window, jumping onto the fire escape, the sun was down but no moon illuminated the night this evening, only the street lamps pierced the gloom of the night.

Silently, she crept down to the street, she prayed she could find him before he took too many victims. Nikolai had become her best hunter, but he was also vicious, he loved to toy with his prey before consuming them. A series of gunfire could be heard to her left and a scream that was quickly silenced, Marie sprinted toward the echoing sound.

As she rounded the corner, she slid to a halt, Nikolai stood in the center of the alley, the body of a young woman limp in his hand. In front of him stood a lone gunman, reloading quickly as the vampire crept forward, another at his side who was a stranger to Marie, had Lorelai begun to create more again?

The older woman hissed at the gunman, her eyes glittering in the lamplight. His hand shook as he took aim at her. "Please don't make me do this." Marie heard him whisper, as the vampire gathered herself and leapt toward him. The sound of the gunshots reverberated down the alley, but the vampire kept coming.

Marie rushed forward as the vampire was about to take down the gunman, she impaled it on the sword, pushing it off with her foot and cutting off the head, a final hiss emitted as she did. She turned toward Nikolai, then regained her battle stance, the lamplight making her blade glow slightly. Nikolai's eyes widened as he recognized the blade of legend, growling, he ran into the darkness.

Behind her she heard a stifled sob as the gunman sank down next to the decapitated body. "Don't touch her." Marie ordered as he reached toward the face of the woman.

"She was my grandmother." He spit at her angrily.

"Your grandmother died the moment she was changed." Marie pulled a lighter from her pocket and threw it at the body, flames engulfing it in seconds. "Hello again, Mark. Come with me."

CHAPTER FORTY FOUR

"Who are you?" Marie demanded as she shoved Mark into the room, Dalil and Roger looking with shock at the new addition toppling in through the window.

"Officer Mark Hunter. How do you know my name? Abducting an officer is against the law." He glared at her and her still bloody sword warily. "Who are they?" He demanded. "More of your hostages?"

Marie moved closer until her face was inches from his. "You saw what chased you, you saw what I did to them. Do you honestly think I'm afraid of your police?" She breathed low and deadly.

Dalil rushed forward, grabbing Mark by the hair, shoving his head sideways, revealing a small tattoo behind his ear. "Where did you get this?" He whispered, his eyes full of shock. Marie glanced at the tattoo, her eyes filled with recognition.

"Markus had the same tattoo." She raised the sword to his throat. "Where did you get that?"

Mark glared at her. "I'm not telling you anything." He spit at her. Roger stepped forward placing a hand on Marie's shoulder.

"Perhaps we can have this conversation over tea, like civilized people. It seems you all have information that needs to be shared in order to complete this puzzle." Roger turned on the coffee pot to warm water, his nose wrinkling slightly but he needed to defuse the situation.

Dalil walked to his bag, he slowly unzipped it, removing

an old leather bound journal. He gestured for everyone to sit as he gently turned the worn pages. Marie pushed Mark away as she sat near the door, eyeing him as he moved to the far side of the room. "Where is your family from?" He asked, not looking up from the journal.

"I don't know." Came the blunt reply. Dalil raised an eyebrow as he looked up at the younger man. Mark blew out a frustrated breath. "I was left on the steps of St. Mary's Church when I was only a few days old. I had the tattoo then, I was wrapped in a blanket with a note asking them to keep me safe, and my name. I was taken to the orphanage and raised there."

"You said the vampire was your grandmother?" Marie asked sharply.

"She was, I was adopted as a child. I never really fit in with my family, but she loved me, in spite of everything." The unfinished tale hung in the air as the group sat in awkward silence. Dalil cleared his throat.

"Well it seems that you are in good company now." He turned the book for them all to see, the same tattoo was drawn on the page. "As I have mentioned before, Ohanna had five children, one went North, one South, one each East and West. My ancestor stayed with her, Marie you are descended from the child of the West, and I believe, Mark, you are a descendant of the child of the North."

"But why did Markus have that tattoo?" Marie questioned.

"I believe I have an answer, but you may not like it. It seems that your husband Markus, was also a descendant of Ohanna's second son, Christos," he held up his hand as Marie began to protest, "I believe he came into your life to be trained by your grandmother."

"No! Markus loved me."

"I'm not denying that, but why did she never train you, or even tell you vampires truly existed?"

"I..." Marie stuttered, at a loss for words, memories flooded back, the day they met, secret conversations she had witnessed, Dalil was right, her husband had been a hunter and she had never even seen it. “She should have trained us both,” she said bitterly, “then everything would have been different.”

“Did Markus have any children before he died?”

“No, but he had a brother, Alasdair, they were never close, he always kept his distance, I thought he was dead so I never searched for him.”

“This tattoo was worn by Christos and by all in his lineage. I lost track of his family many generations ago, it seems they were good at hiding.”

“What of the other children? The East and South? Could any of them have survived?”

“Up until today I would have said no, but perhaps they are better at hiding, than I am at tracking. It seems I’ve gotten old.”

“Wait, hold up. Vampires? Who is Ohanna?

“Ohanna, was the first vampire hunter, mother to all the vampire hunters of the world and you, my boy, are descended from her.”

CHAPTER FORTY FIVE

"I'm a vampire hunter?"

Marie snorted. "No, you are DESCENDED from vampire hunters."

"And yet he faced Nikolai." Roger pointed out.

"And his grandma almost killed him." She caught Roger's eye. "No, I can see what you're thinking. He's not ready, it would be suicide for him to even consider it."

"I'm right here, if you're going to discuss me, at least include me in the conversation." Mark strode across the room, standing in front of them with his arms crossed.

"No, out of the question." Marie pointed her finger at him as she spoke. "You will give me any information you have on the vampires, then you will stay here with them. I will do this alone."

"And how has that been going for you all these years? Doing well? Or have you kept secrets that put your friends and colleagues in danger at every step?" Dalil retorted, his face stormy. "How many people have trusted you and died for it? How many humans have suffered and lost their lives while Lorelai roams free? We have the weapons and the knowledge to destroy her once and for all, let us help you."

"I can't lose anymore, Dalil." She shouted back at him. "I can't lose you."

"Then train us so you won't."

"I have a shop." Three sets of eyes turned to stare at Mark. "What? Those monsters took my grandmother from me, the only family I had in this world, until now it seems. So let's do this. I have a shop I rent to work on cars, it's a hobby to get my mind off work. There's plenty of space to do this 'training'. So, do we have an agreement?" He held out his hand to Marie.

"Lorelai knows I have the sword, Nikolai would have recognized it. We have lost that element of surprise, she will either come to the city to face me or fortify her position. Either way, we have little time. You will face demons unlike any you have ever seen before, you will be lucky if they only kill you. Before you agree, you must know what you are agreeing to."

Mark held her eyes, his hand never wavering. "I'm in." Marie clasped his hand. They quickly grabbed their belongings, as Dalil and Roger left through the door to check out, Marie and Mark carried the weapons down the fire escape, unwilling to draw attention in the lobby.

Quietly, they loaded into the vehicle they had arrived in and drove away, the nicer neighborhood giving way to a seedier atmosphere as Mark drove them to his shop. "It's not the best neighborhood," he apologized, "but I got a good price." Marie watched the homeless, bundled in their belongings to avert the cold.

"It will do."

They pulled the van into the small space and locked the door behind them. It wasn't large, but they had enough room to keep the van safe while maneuvering through their exercises.

"That's odd." Mark mentioned. "There's fewer out tonight, they must have found a warm place to shelter."

Marie pulled the weapons from the van, turning to her students. There was no time for pleasantries anymore. She gave Mark a brief overview of their mission, history lessons would be for another day, now all he needed to learn was how to kill a vampire.

It was a long night, soon Roger and Dalil crawled into the back of the van to get some rest. Marie worried as she watched the two older men's energy flagging so quickly. They would never make it. Mark came at her again, his youth giving him a strength the others did not possess.

He had promise, if only she could have realized his

connection to her earlier, but this was the path they were on, and she was determined to succeed. Time blurred as they continued to practice, food was delivered at random, sleep came in spurts. Marie knew they had to leave soon.

Outside the sound of a bus stopping could be heard and a commotion. Marie walked to the door, she peeked out into the darkness, noticing the homeless quickly walking to the bus that had parked near them.

"Free food and shelter, to get out of this terrible cold."

She could hear the little man in white speaking to the people. He appeared to be from the local outreach, until he turned toward her.

"I know him." She whispered to Mark. "It's time to go."

CHAPTER FORTY SIX

Lorelai threw her head back and laughed, all the frustration of the past few weeks melted away.

"My Queen, she has the sword. I saw it, it glowed in her hands."

"And you ran away, my bravest hunter ran away." Nikolai hung his head, his shame oozing from his body, Lorelai could almost smell it.

"To warn you, My Queen, I will return to the city, I will bring her lifeless body to you."

"I should kill you for your failure and cowardice, but you truly do bring me good tidings." Confusion crossed Nikolai's face.

"But the sword, it can kill you."

"And it can kill her. Finally, after all these centuries, I will be free of that pest. I will destroy her, and Ohanna's legacy will finally be ended. No one can stop us now." Her laughter became maniacal as she saw the downfall of Marie, her broken body lying in a pool of blood.

"I will leave at once to retrieve the sword."

"No, you will stay. She will come to us. Tell the little gremlins to make sure they are seen as they gather more sacrifices to wake the rest of the nest. She will follow them, then we shall destroy her." Lorelai looked out the window, for the past few days her minions had been gathering homeless from the streets of New York, bringing them here under the cover of darkness. No one would miss the filth from the street, but she would cherish them. They were, after all, essential to her plan.

"Yes, My Queen." Nikolai bowed as he turned to leave the

room.

"Nikolai? Make sure this new batch is cleaned before they are sent below. Even hogs are washed before they're sent to slaughter."

Nikolai left to complete his duties as Lorelai continued to stare out the window, her reflection in the dark glass gloated at her. All these years, finally an end was in sight. All Ohanna's scheming had come to nothing, Lorelai would win at last. The sword would be hers, she would strike down her foe, she would destroy the only weapon that could take her life, and she would rule the Earth until the end of time.

Lorelai tossed her hair over her shoulder, she smirked at the people huddled together in the cold. She should go down to greet her guests before introducing them to their fate. Slowly she descended the staircase into the main room of the farmhouse. The newest arrivals had begun to trickle in.

"Welcome friends." She called with a smile as she stepped onto the porch. "Please follow Nikolai as we have warm showers prepared. Then we shall feast."

A little boy came up to her, his dirty hair falling in his face, a small bruise was showing on his cheek. "Thank you miss, everyone says we're worthless."

Lorelai caressed his filthy cheek, her smile becoming brighter to hide her disgust. "Oh, but my little cupcake, you're everything to me." He hugged her tight before running off to follow the others, she stopped one of her minions before he returned to the bus to retrieve another load. "Make sure you save the children." She said absently.

"My Queen?"

She jerked her head toward him and raised her brow. "The most pure blood has always gone to the royalty on the night of the sacrifice. The children will awaken the highest ranking in the coven. Now I need to change, I can smell his stench on me."

The one she always teased for being grumpy sneered. He hated getting the dregs, the foul diseased blood or tainted by whatever they put in their body. For centuries, he and his brothers had served her, done her bidding without question, yet still she treated them little better than garbage.

What would happen to her plan if he decided to change sides? If those who had always held her up, suddenly were no longer there? He grabbed his radio, moving away from the house, this message needed no witnesses.

"Make sure you're seen as Nikolai ordered you, but meet me once you arrive. I have a plan."

CHAPTER FORTY SEVEN

The occupants of the van were silent as they drove slowly behind the bus, it was completely full now as it turned out of town.

"Are they still in the town?" Mark wondered aloud.

"What town?"

"My grandmothers town. When I visited and discovered the slaughter, my grandmother said it was vampires. She said I shouldn't be there, I assume that's why the large one came after me. But the town burned."

"Then she must be close. Slow down, we don't want to make it obvious we're following them. Her minions are clever."

"It will be hard to hide the farther out we go. Some of these areas don't have many options as far as directions to travel. It would be odd that we would be going to the same random rural area."

"True, but I have no way to track them, just do your best."

Mark slowed the van, keeping the tail lights of the bus in his distant vision. They all held their breath as they disappeared from view for a moment as a dip in the road moved the bus from their sight.

Marie opened her bag, looking at the small glass bottle within. As the last of her line, she had thought to leave the bottle to Roger, with everything else. Now, she had discovered she had more kin than she realized.

She glanced at Dalil as he focused on the darkness and

the taillights in the distance. In her heart, she had little faith in him surviving this night. She so wanted to save him, to live out his dream of enjoying his chair and his pipe, relaxing together in triumph, but she knew he would stay with her until the end.

This little bottle could save him, if they had time, but their time had run out. Now it would fall to Mark, if he survived, one part of herself that she could pass on to the next generation. She took a slip of paper, hurriedly writing a brief note, then wrapping it around the bottle and slipping it back into her bag. Now was not the time.

Hours passed as they continued to follow the bus, nerves began to churn in Marie's stomach as she wondering if they still followed their prey. The dim light indicating low fuel flashed on the dashboard.

"We need to stop soon. There's a station not far ahead. With luck we can catch up before they turn off."

Marie nodded tensely as her foot began to jiggle, they didn't have time for this. The bright lights of the small gas station came into view and Mark pulled up to the single pump.

"Ah, well I need a moment. If you'll excuse me." Roger said as he moved to leave the vehicle. He froze at Marie's fierce look. "Actually, I think I'll hold it."

The minutes seemed to go in reverse as Marie could hear the slow workings of the pump outside, with excruciating agony. At last, she could hear Mark replace the cap and return to the drivers seat. The engine revved and the tires squealed slightly as he sped forward, no longer interested in subterfuge. The hunt was on, they had lost time and he aimed to make it up.

No taillights gleamed in the distance, no bus could be seen as they sped along. He slammed his hand into the steering wheel, angry with himself for losing them, he was better then this. A dim glow illuminated the horizon as an open gate came into view on their right.

"Should we investigate?"

"Something big is happening. Turn off the lights, we can drive partway, then go the rest of the way on foot. We still have some time before the sun rises, so we aren't safe out here yet." Marie agreed as the van turned toward the illuminated farmhouse.

"If the sun rises, they can't be out, we could burn the house with them in it."

"Unless she created a nest underground, like in Italy." Interjected Dalil. "Underground, she would have no weakness, though we would be at her mercy."

"We fight, no matter the obstacles." Marie pointed toward a small grove of trees, instructing Mark to park behind them, a cover in case another bus came. As they gathered their weapons for the walk to the farmhouse, Marie stopped Roger. "Please stay, if we fail, someone will need to warn the humans."

Roger began to protest, his desire to help overriding his logic. "The more of us there are, the better chance we stand."

"And if we all fall, who will protect the humans?" She handed him her bag. "Keep this safe for me. I want Mark to have it." Roger pulled her close, hugging her tightly, fearing this would be the final time he would see her face, hear her voice.

"Go, be safe, my friend."

"I want to be buried next to Ohanna."

"When the time comes." Tears slid unchecked down his cheeks as he watched them walk away.

The three hunters walked quietly toward the light, getting on their bellies, crawling to the top of a small bank so they could observe the gathering. In the center of the yard was the bus, the gathered humans milled around as others directed them to different areas.

"Welcome Huntress, we've been expecting you."

CHAPTER FORTY EIGHT

Marie's blade rang as she pulled it from its sheath.

"No wait, please, I offer aid." The minion cowered, his hands raised in surrender.

"And why would you help me?" Marie spat out, raising her blade, preparing to strike.

"For centuries, I have been her slave, treated as garbage, watching her take favorites who do nothing, while I am abused if I do not do everything I am told. I am tired of this eternal life. I could ask that you kill me alone, but I know what she has planned for this world, I want to help you stop her before I die."

Marie lowered her weapon slowly, she had always seen this creature and his brothers in the background of her eternal dance with Lorelai. She had thought him to be a devoted follower, one who would lay down his life for his queen, but Marie could see the anguish of a hundred lifetimes of anger and betrayal behind his eyes. He may not be her ally, but he was also no longer Lorelai's slave, for this brief moment, she knew she could trust him.

"Take me to her and I will end your suffering, to allow you the peace you deserve."

The man nodded, a look of relief flitted across his face, the only indication that he was at peace with his decision. He motioned for the group to follow him as he made his way around the outside of the yard, slipping through the bushes and mounds, ancient evidence of bodies that had been buried throughout the years.

Their presence went unnoticed or ignored by the vampires in the yard, who were busy with the new arrivals, preparing them for the ceremony to awaken the remainder of the coven. The ceremony would take place just before dawn, in the dead hours as the night ended and the day began. They would spend the day in the nest, feeding on the humans they had gathered, preparing to unleash their might on the world. Unless Marie could stop them.

They slipped around to the back of the farmhouse, entering undetected. Marie heard a soft click as the man locked the door behind her and his brothers emerged from the adjoining room. Marie tensed, was this a trap?

"The queen is strong, but we don't want her to call the others to her aid. My brothers will stay here to guard the doors, they will lock the door to the nest once we enter. Once you have defeated her, you will be able to open it from the inside with this key."

Marie took the metal key, handing it to Mark. "Keep this safe for me." She smiled as she turned to her guide. "Your brothers will die if we don't open the door before dawn."

"They will die when you succeed. We are not blind to our fate, we know we are tied to the life of the queen."

Mark looked confused for a moment, but followed Marie as she moved toward the sitting room. The man held up his hand as he neared the door, motioning them to stop and move back.

"My queen, the van was last spotted at the gas station close to here. They should find us soon."

"Make sure they do." Came the icy voice from beyond the door. "I want this finished tonight."

"Yes, my Queen."

Marie could barely see the hidden door open and Lorelai descend the stairs to the nest. She gripped her sword but the man put his hand on hers to stop her.

"Wait until she's in the nest. Everyone else is outside, she will be alone, with no one to call for aid."

"Thank you." Marie looked into his sad eyes. "What's your name? After all these centuries I've never known."

"Jo... Johannes," came the stuttering reply, "it was part of her hold over me, to show me my place, she never allowed my name to be spoken."

"Thank you, Johannes."

"It is I who should thank you, for allowing my name to be spoken once more before I die."

Slowly the group descended the stairs, the closure of the door and lock echoed around them as they continued into the inky darkness, the thin light at the base of the stairs beckoning them.

An evil laugh greeted them as they reached the bottom. There stood Lorelai, bathed in light, a small body at her feet, staring into oblivion with lifeless eyes.

"Hello Huntress, I've been waiting for you." She smirked. She stood casually, her face holding a secret only she found humorous as a masked man walked from behind her, blood dripping from his mouth. "I don't believe you've met my husband."

CHAPTER FORTY NINE

Marie exhaled slowly, adjusting her sword, preparing to destroy the vampires. Lorelai's laughter filled the room as the man removed his mask, Marie felt the wind sucked out of her as she fell to her knees. "I believe you two know each other."

"Markus?" Marie cried, tears streaming down her face, her breath coming in gasps. Her chest felt as though Lorelai had punched through her. "You made my husband into a monster?"

"Oh no, my dear, YOU made your husband into a monster." Lorelai laughed cruelly as she moved toward Marie. "When you attacked me, my blood covered him and entered his mouth, allowing him to live. I never would have turned him, but once I found him alive, I healed him from the wounds that YOU inflicted by burning him in that building. I saved him, I gave him this life, now he will be my weapon to destroy you."

"Markus is dead," Dalil called from behind her, "this creature is just his carcass, controlled by this demon to distract you. Get up and fight Marie, avenge Markus, and destroy Lorelai."

Lorelai smirked. "Do you really believe you can destroy me, old man? How very amusing. Do you even know who I am?" She raised her arms above her head, the ground shook slightly as she began to softly glow. "I am Selene, Titan goddess of the moon, sister to the sun god Helios, and goddess of the dawn Eos. You cannot kill me."

"Selene? Of course, it all makes sense now." Dalil muttered. "Where is your master then? Where is Ambrogio?"

"Ambrogio," Lorelai sneered, "is not my master. He is a fool. My life was perfect, then he came in and destroyed it all, cursing me to this eternal hell." She paced angrily away from Marie, momentarily forgetting her purpose of the evening. "I thought he loved me, but for that love I lost my immortality, I lost my family, I was banished to live alone on the moon, watching as those I loved lived and died, while I could do nothing but whisper to them from afar.

I had to watch as that betrayer, Ohanna, lived her perfect life, destroying the children Ambrogio made for me, his only gift to me that mattered. So I embraced my curse, I left the moon and surrendered my soul, I became the Queen of the Vampires. I took the name Lorelai from the legends of the siren, drawing in sailors to their doom, I became the doom of humanity. I took Ambrogio and I imprisoned him, I wanted to kill him, but like you, I am bound to him. You think you are only bound to me as my blood made you, but all vampires are bound to him. He is the first.

I keep him barely alive, no one will ever find him, no one will release him. He will stay in the purgatory I have created for him for eternity." Lorelai laughed again, her eyes had become crazed. "I created the stories that turned humanity against you, not solely because I hated you for hunting me, but as a penance for being the descendant of Ohanna.

I guided history, every leader who ever mattered, every scholar, author, scientist. They were all under my control! Cleopatra, the brothers Grimm, da Vinci, Roosevelt, anyone who created this world is there because I guided them."

"Hitler?" Mark smirked.

"No, he was all yours. I worked to grow my flock, not destroy it." Lorelai said in disgust. "And now, my plans have been realized, all I have to do is kill you. By morning, the rest of my coven will be awakened and we will take over the world. The humans will serve us as food or slaves. You have lost."

CHAPTER FIFTY

"No!" Marie screamed, rising from the floor, swinging her sword in front of her. "We will never lose. Ohanna was given this sword as a way to destroy you, as an apology to all human kind for the gods part in creating the demons you call vampires. Once I kill you, this will all be over."

"Markus, kill her." Lorelai screamed, her eyes wide with rage. He turned toward Marie, his dark eyes burning into hers.

"No." He said flatly. "I would never hurt her, she is my light in the darkness, my only star in the sky. I allied with you solely to see her face again, to help her defeat you. I will not fight for you, I am prepared to die."

"Then die you shall." Lorelai screamed as she grabbed him and threw him toward Marie. Marie felt the sword impale him as she tried to move out of the way, she was too late, the sword would destroy any vampire.

"No." She cried as she lowered him to the floor. His hand caressed her face.

"I have only ever loved you." He said as his body went limp, the light faded from his eyes.

"We end this." Marie wiped the tears from her eyes and faced Lorelai. "Lorelai, Selene, demon, Queen, I don't care what you call yourself. You will die."

"Come this way." Johannes whispered to Dalil. "I know where he lies." The pair slipped around the room, down a dark path, unseen by the battling women. The sounds of battle followed them as they reached a locked door. "Behind this door is Ambrogio, we must destroy him."

"I have no weapon, when the battle is finished I will have

Mark kill him."

"If we kill him now, they will not need to fight."

"Betrayer!" Came a scream of rage from behind them, Johannes was thrown into the wall, crashing through it, laying crumpled next to the stone casket.

"Johannes." Dalil climbed over the stones, hurrying to his aid.

"Go, warn Marie there is another here." Johannes struggled to his feet, his leg obviously broken, pushing Dalil onto the casket as Nikolai attacked again. Dalil felt a sting in his arm as warm blood spilled from the cut and onto the casket. "Go!"

Dalil ran from the room, the sounds of Nikolai beating Johannes, sickening him. His lungs burned as he ran back to the main room.

"Marie, Nikolai is here. Finish her." Dalil yelled as heavy footsteps came down the hall, a hand crashed into his back and he flew through the air. Mark turned to face the new threat, the spear singing through the air as he stood back to back with Marie.

They could hear banging as the vampires upstairs tried to break through the door to the nest. "We're running out of time." Mark said as the pair circled, watching the vampires carefully.

"Duck!" Marie cried, pulling Mark to the side as Nikolai bowled past them, missing the pair as they rolled out of the way, catapulting himself into Lorelai. "Now!" Marie lifted her sword and drove it into Lorelai's heart. "Die Lorelai, Queen of Darkness, and take your spawn with you." Marie spat out.

Lorelai chuckled. "Only if you come with me." Marie swung her sword, she removed Lorelai's head, falling to the ground as the head rolled across the floor. Dalil crawled to her, cradling her as she struggled to breathe.

"Finally, it's over." She smiled. "I wish we could have enjoyed it as you wanted to, with your chair and your pipe.

"We will always be together." He said, softly kissing her forehead as he closed her eyes.

"I didn't think it would be so fast."

"She was tied to her, as all Lorelai's creations were, now they are all gone. Take up the sword, you are the only one left to continue our family. Place Marie next to Ohanna, and me next to Marie. It's what she would have wanted."

"You're coming with me."

"No," Dalil wheezed, his eyes hazy, lifting his shirt and revealing his broken chest, the rib puncturing the skin, "I go with Marie. Find Roger, he will teach you everything." Dalil laid his head on Marie's forehead, allowing his life to slip from his body. Their family had succeeded, their mission was over, Mark would destroy Ambrogio, had he told him? He couldn't remember. "Dest... Destr..."

Dalil's final breath left his body as Mark picked up the sword. He would retrieve the van and take his family home, reunite them with Ohanna, then ensure the tomb was never opened again. He took the key from his pocket and opened the door, the light of morning burning the vampire bodies in the yard to ash.

He smiled, a new beginning, a new life as The Huntsman. The children of Lorelai may be gone, but there could still be children of Ambrogio alive and if they were, he would be ready for them. Mark slung the spear over his shoulder as he began walking down the road to the van, whistling softly.

* * * *

The blood on the casket had begun to coagulate as it slowly slid across the rock and into the opening. Slowly, it dripped onto the creature within and in the darkness, red eyes opened.

The End

Made in the USA
Middletown, DE
23 August 2024